DID BLACK PATENT LEATHER SHOES OFFER A VISION OF PARADISE?

Could the gleaming surface of feminine footwear *really* reflect upward to mirror a girl's most intimate charms?

This was just one of many burning questions confronting Eddie Ryan, growing to young manhood in the early '60s, and discovering the facts of life and love with his friends in a mid-America trembling with change.

This was the way it was then—the dreams and dilemmas, the back seat fumbling and the breathless fulfillments, the black-and-white realities and the technicolor dreams— in a hilarious, heartwarming, sometimes heartbreaking novel that makes it all happen again now.

"The author follows his *The Last Catholic in America* with another winner . . . You'll never forget it."
—*Publishers Weekly*

Do Black Patent Leather Shoes Really Reflect Up?

A novel by John R. Powers

FAWCETT POPULAR LIBRARY • NEW YORK

Just Call Me Hardrock, Randy

Acknowledgments

Mary, Margo Powers for that night at the roller rink. John F. and June R. Powers. Gay and Dr. Joseph V. Gioioso for their contributions. Joey, Randy Marie, Danielle. Dr. Martin J. Maloney of Northwestern University and Bill Wright for both their professional and personal assistance.

DO BLACK PATENT LEATHER SHOES REALLY REFLECT UP?

Published by Fawcett Popular Library, a unit of CBS Publications, the Consumer Publishing Division of CBS Inc., by arrangement with Henry Regnery Company

ISBN: 0-445-08490-1

Printed in the United States of America

First Fawcett Popular Library Printing: October 1976

21   20   19   18   17   16   15   14   13

1

For twelve straight years I had been on this earth when, for no apparent reason, God decided to stick me by allowing me to become a teen-ager.

The first six months of being thirteen weren't hard to take because they were spent in the eighth grade. When you're sitting atop the world of grammar school, nothing can go wrong. But within days of graduating from St. Bastion Grammar School on Chicago's South Side, my body began disintegrating in a series of slow explosions.

Early one summer morning, as I got out of bed, I casually went to scratch my forehead. But instead of finding my forehead, my fingers landed on something that felt like a gravel road. That could mean only one thing. I raced out of the bedroom to my private place of worship, the mirror above the bathroom sink. As I stared into the mirror, I saw at least twenty pudgy red pimples staring back at me.

I remembered what my mother had told my older sister about pimples when my older sister had started getting them. They were caused by two things, said my mother, sweets and dirt.

My mind jumped back to the night before when I had eaten a Snickers bar for dessert. No, that couldn't have been it. A Snickers bar might give somebody two or three pimples, but twenty?

It had to be dirt. My mother was always telling me how cruddy I was.

I didn't want to look at them. I turned off the bathroom light (fortunately pimples don't glow in the dark) and spent the next hour and a half washing my face. When I turned the bathroom light back on, I discovered that the only thing that looks worse on your forehead than twenty pimples is twenty clean pimples. Clean pimples look shinier and a lot more disgusting.

It was time to be terrified. I was quite aware of the fact that pimples were nothing to play around with. If they got bad enough, they'd scar you for life. A perfect label on your face, announcing to anyone who cared to know, THIS PERSON NEVER WASHED HIS FACE AND ATE EVERYTHING HE WASN'T SUPPOSED TO WHEN HE WAS A TEEN-AGER.

My mother was a very neat type of person, but one thing she never managed to clean out was the medicine cabinet. Every three weeks, she'd take all the jars, boxes, and bottles out of the medicine cabinet, scrub down the inside of the cabinet, and then put all the jars, boxes, and bottles right back in. When I was a kid I had a couple of cases of constipation, separated by years of bowel stability, that were cured from the same bottle of castor oil. As my hand groped around inside the medicine cabinet, I knew that the jar I wanted was still in there somewhere.

When my older sister had developed pimple problems, she had used Nolsteen Face Cream on them. I don't know if the stuff helped or not, but her pimples went away. My sister, of course, did everything else my mother told her to do, like staying away from sweets and keeping her face clean.

That was when my sister was in grammar school and she was still trying to pattern her life after the Blessed Virgin Mary, who had a strong reputation for being sweet and pure. There was no way my sister was going to excel in the first category and I think she knew it. She could be sweet to nuns, adults, and a few of her friends, maybe with little kids, too, but that was about it. So she tried to be big in the second category. Knowing the way my sister thought, she probably felt that a pimple on her forehead was a real threat to her purity image.

My groping hand finally found the blue jar of Nolsteen Face Cream behind a dead tube of toothpaste and an unopened jar of after-shave lotion, which was within a few years of reaching heirloom antiquity.

It took ten minutes of pounding, twisting, and swearing to get the top of the jar off. Some of the face cream had dried and molded around the edges of the cap. The jar was only half full. But the cream, instead of being white and soft, was brownish and as solid as rock.

I poured a few drops of warm water into the jar, which softened the Nolsteen Face Cream, and stirred the facial stew with my finger. Then I scooped some of the glop out of the jar, slapped it on my forehead, and smeared it all over my pimples. As I watched in the mirror, the Nolsteen Face Cream instantly dehydrated, turned grayish black, crusted, and fell, in one large lump, into the bathroom sink. My pimples were shinier than ever.

I went out and bought another jar of Nolsteen Face Cream. It helped a little. After I applied the cream from the new jar, some of the pimples didn't seem to glow quite as brightly.

But all of that was just the opening skirmish. The war of pimples had hardly begun. It would be years before I was to emerge victorious. The campaign would be a costly one. Thousands of candy bars, cupcakes, dishes of ice cream, French fries, and Cokes would go unconsumed. The pores on my face would absorb dozens of bottles of Nolsteen Face Cream, tubes of Fresh Air Complexion Cream, and lemon-soaked pads. For the duration of the teen-age years, my fingers would automatically go on pimple patrol every time I got near a mirror and almost every other second that I wasn't occupied with doing something else.

Sometimes, for instance, I'd be sitting in school, doing nothing except sliding my fingers across my face, when I'd suddenly touch something that would send pounds of pain pulsating through my skin. It would feel as if my finger had just pushed a nail through my face. But as soon as I got to a mirror, I wouldn't be able to see any pimples in the area from where the pain was pouring. That was the worst type of pimple, the one you couldn't see, for the moment at least. It was still on its way up and hadn't quite reached skin level.

For the next few days, that pimple would be a land mine on my fingers' pimple patrols. They would forget it was there until one of them glided across it. Then pain would flare out from that unseen pimple in eighty million directions. Worse yet, I was already feeling ashamed over a pimple that I hadn't even seen yet. Such pimples always surfaced on weekends.

During the final months of eighth grade, I had noticed that small lumps were beginning to grow under both of my knees. I didn't think they were anything to be alarmed about. A couple of weeks before I had become aware of the growths, one of the parish priests had come into our eighth-grade classroom to talk to us about "growing up." He said that within the next few years we could expect many changes to occur within our bodies. I just figured that the lumps under my knees were examples of what he was talking about.

A few days after graduation I noticed that the lumps were becoming extremely sensitive. If I bumped them against anything, they'd just about kill me with pain.

One Saturday morning my mother was vacuuming in the living room. She had the furniture pulled out when I accidentally walked into the cocktail table, which was exactly lumps-high. My mother thought it was rather strange that I should nearly pass out from the pain of walking into a cocktail table, so it was off to the family doctor.

Its official name, according to our doctor, was Osgood Schlatter's disease. There was only one cure for it. You had to rest the leg; that is, put it in a cast. I had to wear a cast on one leg for six weeks, then have it removed and wear another cast on the other leg for six more weeks.

I told almost no one about what was really wrong with my legs. At first I mentioned it to a few friends, but they just looked at me like I was nuts. What a dumb name, "Osgood Schlatter." Most physical afflictions at least sound respectable. "He has a compound fracture." "He has a vitamin deficiency." When you hear stuff like that, you sort of feel sorry for the person involved. But "He has Osgood Schlatter's disease" sounds stupid. Who ever heard of a disease that sounds like it was named after a guy who played left field for the New York Yankees?

I just told people I had broken my leg. When, a few weeks later, they saw me limping around on the other leg, I told them I had broken that one, too. That might have seemed dumb to them but not as dumb as the truth would have.

It wasn't too bad, walking around with a cast on my leg. The cast started just above my ankle and ended a few inches above my knee so I could fit my pants leg over it. The only extremely annoying part of wearing it was that when the weather got hot, the skin beneath the cast itched like mad.

There were only a few times when my stiff leg really embarrassed me. When I went to Mass on Sunday, people would stare at me because I'd never kneel when I was supposed to. I'd just sit there with my stiff leg laying across the kneeler. Everyone around me probably thought that I was terrifically lazy or something.

Another time I was on a crowded bus when this man standing above me tried to put some change back in his pocket. As he did so, he accidentally dropped a quarter on my lap. The quarter's edge hit the cast perfectly and bounced almost all the way back up to him. You could hear it "ping" all over the bus. He apologized to me at least thirty times. He must have thought I had a wooden leg.

A few kids mocked me about it. Not many, though. Gordon Lester was the only kid who developed his teasing tactics into a full-time job. Lester was a tall, gawkish sort of kid who gave every indication of growing up to be a dishwasher, and not a very good one at that. Whenever he saw me, he'd start mocking me and calling me

"Chester," which was the name of a stiff-legged character on the television show "Gunsmoke."

An easygoing friend of mine, Tom Lanner, got Osgood Schlatter's disease about the same time that I did. I had a newspaper route then. Since I couldn't ride a bike, I had to walk the route. Lanner came over a few times to help me. That was when Gordon Lester really got his laughs.

Lanner and I, both stiff-legged, would hobble down the street together. No matter how we did it, we still looked insane. If we limped at the same time, we felt as if we were doing a comedy routine. If we limped out of step, we had a tough time talking to one another, since our heads kept bobbing past each other like two horses on a merry-go-round.

Gordon Lester would be right behind us, laughing on every limp. He didn't bother Lanner or me too much. He wasn't doing it to be mean. Lester was just a very simple-minded person who grabbed his giggles when he could.

When Gordon Lester first started laughing at us, I tried to keep him at a distance by threatening him with the unknown future. "Keep it up, Lester," I'd say, "and some day I'll be laughing at you. Someday, something's going to happen to you and then I'm gonna laugh my ass off."

That only made Gordon Lester chuckle more, so I gave up and tried to ignore him. Not that I believed what I was saying. I knew that nothing was going to happen to Lester to even out the score. Life never works out so neatly. But that time it did.

Not more than a couple of weeks after I had the last cast taken off my leg, Gordon Lester was messing around the foundation of a new building that was going up in the neighborhood, fell in, and broke his leg in four different places.

Being basically a decent guy, I didn't mock Gordon Lester the way he had mocked me. I didn't ridicule the way he walked or call him "Chester." I couldn't. He was in the hospital, in traction, for three weeks and then his family moved out of the neighborhood.

Midway through the summer, with one leg in a cast, the other still lumpy, and my face looking like a miniature golf course, my voice began going crazy. Its lunatic leanings would become most obvious when I'd try to sing around the house, which I often did when there was no one else at home.

My throat would be merrily molesting some song when, without warning, my voice would break stride and leap up two or three octaves, scramble around for an instant and then plunge straight down to at least three octaves below where it had originally been. For a while, whistling was also something of a problem.

Although most of my anatomy was busily going bananas that summer, the top of my head was beginning to regain its composure. In the early months of eighth grade, I had developed a case of dandruff unlike any the world had ever seen before. My father thought that maybe the dandruff was caused by my hair being too long so he talked me into getting a baldy sour. All that did was make my head look like the top of a snow-capped mountain. Our family doctor later informed my mother that the dandruff was caused by nervousness. Gradually, though, the dandruff had begun to clear up to the point that now, if I peered very closely into the

12

mirror and parted my hair just right, I might see a glimpse of my scalp.

During those summer months I was also beginning to smell—a sure sign, according to my Uncle Frank, that I was nudging into manhood. That was the way Uncle Frank defined masculinity, by smell. According to the rest of the family, Uncle Frank had been a "man" ever since he had been old enough to refuse to hold a bar of soap.

Somewhere in all those years I spent in grammar school I remembered some nun telling us that every seven years our body cells created a whole new body. During those summer months of being thirteen, I was beginning to feel that my only hope of saving my body from self-destruction was if I could reach my twentieth birthday.

It was now the middle of August. I was within two weeks of starting high school, yet I had very little idea of what it was. I've always had that problem. Sometimes I'll look back on a particular phase of my existence and I'll think about what came up right after it. Then I'll wonder why I didn't realize what was coming so that I could better prepare myself for it. I've never been able to see around the corners of life. Maybe it's impossible for anybody to do it. I don't know.

I was aware of some of the things about high school, since I knew quite a few people who had already gone there. My older sister was in high school. I knew, therefore, by observing her, that although grammar school homework took up only a snack tray, high school homework was a full dining room table project. I also realized that there weren't "grades" in high school but rather "years" like "Freshman Year" and "Sophomore Year."

My sister tried to convince me that high school was a place where you had to work yourself to death. She never got home from school until six or seven o'clock. She was always staying late to do extra work. I didn't believe her when she told me high school was that tough. My sister was the kind of person who loved to kill herself doing anything. She could work up a sweat brushing her teeth.

The high school kids who lived in my parish, St. Bastion, thought they were pretty cool. Each one would walk around the neighborhood in his high school jacket with the cream-covered sleeves as if God had just offered him a deed to the world and he had turned it down.

Even if a high school kid didn't own a high school jacket, you could still tell he was in high school by the way he carried himself around. There were two basic "high school" walks; the "Shit, Man, I'm Cool Walk" and the "I'm Big Stuff Walk."

The "Shit, Man, I'm Cool Walk" was performed with the head bowed, shoulders slumped, hands hanging casually from the pants pockets, side or back ones, feet shuffling, and a sneer on the face. The overall effect of all this was a "Proud Bum" look.

The "I'm Big Stuff Walk" was done with the head held extremely high, the shoulders stiff, the hands jammed into the pockets, but with the elbows straight and the entire body leaning slightly forward. In this walk, when a kid took a step forward he would push himself straight up on the balls of his feet. If a high school kid properly executed the "I'm Big Stuff Walk," when he moved down the street he would look like a slightly tipsy, weak-springed pogo stick.

When I was in the lower grades of grammar school, I used to watch the high school kids play basketball in the school yard, their jackets piled in a heap behind the post. The only time they'd talk to me was when one of them missed a pass and the ball would go bouncing across the school yard.

"Hey, kid, get the ball for us, will you?"

"Sure, sure." I'd run after the ball, grab it, and run back with it. Then I'd fling the basketball back to the biggest guy as hard as I could.

"Thanks, kid."

"Yeah, sure."

Sometimes I'd see a high school kid coming out of Russie's Restaurant, jingling the change in his pocket. Grammar school kids never went to Russie's. Even an order of fries cost a quarter. Besides, Russie didn't like grammar school kids. He believed that when grammar school kids got hungry they should go to a delicatessen, not a restaurant.

If a high school kid I knew walked by me on the street, he'd occasionally say "hello." Not actually "hello." He'd just sort of grunt in my direction. He might not even do that. But if he was walking along with a group of other guys, he'd totally ignore me. People always think they're hotshots if they're with a crowd of other people who think they're hotshots, too.

A few times when I was little, like in second or third grade, one of them would come along, shooting the bull with some girl, and as he walked by me he'd pat me on the head. That really enraged me. But I was too small to do anything about it.

The Catholic school that I attended, St. Bastion, was a bore. All we ever did was write in our workbooks, do

15

arithmetic problems on notebook paper, using a ruler of course, or read silently or out loud from one of our textbooks.

Occasionally, to break the monotony, you'd pretend that you had to go to the washroom. One kid would raise his hand and if the nun gave him permission to go to the washroom, then a few minutes later another kid would raise his hand. It would just keep going like that. The nun must have thought that all of our kidneys were connected.

Actually I only went to seven years of grammar school. In the first week of second grade, I got sick and spent the rest of the year at home. When I came back to school the following September, the nun took one look at me, decided I was tall enough, and sent me on to third grade.

Most of the nuns didn't seem to have much use for me, maybe because I never did my homework. Well, almost never. During the first seven grades of grammar school I did it twice, once in fourth grade and once in sixth. I remember those two days quite distinctly. They were the only days of grammar school that I didn't sit in terror waiting for the nun to deliver the words that always came. "All right, those who didn't do their homework, stand."

My grades in grammar school weren't too good, either. Often the nuns, rather than giving me a "U" for "Unsatisfactory" on my report card, would instead give me an "S" that stood for "Satisfactory for this child's ability." A nice way of saying I was a moron.

The nuns did that deliberately because they knew an "S" would get everybody even madder at me than a "U" would. After each report card day that was smudged with a batch of "U's," my father would threaten to kill me, my mother wouldn't allow me to watch television, my older sister would ignore me, and if the dog went in the house, he'd let loose in my room.

But there was no such thing as failure when you became an eighth grader. Eighth graders are the gods of any grammar school. Like gods, they have no equals. When I got into eighth grade, I suddenly began doing all of my homework and getting reasonable grades. Most of my dumb friends began doing well, too. The giddiness of wrapping up grammar school somehow does things to your head.

During the final days of eighth grade, the nun warned us that we should spend our upcoming summer vacation getting ready for high school. She even told a few kids who were weak in English that they should read their English grammar books during the vacation.

Every now and then a nun would make it so obvious that she was crazy, like when she asked someone to read an English grammar book during the summer vacation.

No one in the class took the nun's warnings seriously, except maybe a few girls who took everything the nun said seriously. Nuns were very "get ready" people. "Get ready for lunch," "get ready for a spelling test," "get ready for the principal's visit," "get ready for prayers," "get ready for Heaven."

The vast majority of Catholic high schools in the Chicago area were not coeducational. The Church hierarchy probably felt that both sexes could concentrate better on their school work if the other sex wasn't around. Most likely the Church would try to get your mind off food by starving you to death.

There were about five Catholic boys' high schools within commuting distance of my parish. I had decided to attend Bremmer High School, which was only two miles away, simply because it was the closest. Tom Lanner also hoped to go there, but as late as April of eighth grade he still wasn't sure that he could do it.

Bremmer charged a few hundred dollars a year for tuition, as did the other Catholic high schools in the area. The average Catholic family, in order to handle the expenses of a Catholic education, had to give up some of the frills of the finer life, such as a later model car or a few inches on the new television screen. But with Lanner, tuition money was a major problem.

He and his younger sister lived with their aunt, who, besides being very nice, was also very old and poor. His parents were dead, at least his mother was. Lanner wasn't too sure about what had happened to his father. Since seventh grade, Tom had been working part-time jobs to bring money into the house. There was only a week remaining for high school registration when one of Lanner's uncles came across with some money that, combined with what Tom had already saved, totaled enough to pay for the tuition at Bremmer.

Felix Lindor, better known as "Felix the Filth Fiend Lindor," proud possessor of the world's dirtiest mind, was going to Bremmer High School in September. Felix had a mind that worked like the floor of a livery stable. Anyone who knew him for even a few minutes could easily envision Felix's eventual epitaph: "Buried Under Six Feet of What He Loved Most."

Felix Lindor and I had been members of the same boy scout troop for a few months when we were in the sixth grade. Felix had that unique ability to be dirty under any circumstances. On the Saturday morning of our annual crosstown hike, we were all asked to meet in St. Bastion Church so that we could, as a troop, go to confession and then attend Mass and receive Holy Communion.

The confessionals had small red lights above each door. When someone knelt down on the kneeler inside the confessional, the red light would flash on, indicating that the confessional was now occupied. The purpose of the red light was to deter anyone from accidentally opening the door in the middle of someone else's confession.

With folded hands and solemn face, Felix Lindor glided into the confessional and closed the door. The red light flashed on. Then it flashed off. It flashed on again. Felix was apparently getting on and off the kneeler. All of us being boy scouts, we realized that he wasn't just flashing a red light on and off, but was sending us a message in Morse code. The message suggested self-procreation.

A few weeks later, Felix was asked to resign from the scouts when he was caught making obscene knots.

Felix Lindor was the social seer of the eighth grade. When one became an eighth grader, two forms of social behavior were virtually mandatory. First, you had to learn how to walk around the neighborhood for hours and arrive at nowhere. Secondly, you had to develop the ability to reply incoherently whenever an adult threw a question at you. For instance, if you were walking out the door and your mother asked you where you were going, you would say, "You know, ma, I'm going over to ..." at which point you would drag your hand across your lips, shredding the remainder of what you said into muffled mumblings. The first few times you tried it on an adult, he or she would often insist that you speak the language. But after being properly conditioned, the adult would accept such utterings as communication.

Everyone in the neighborhood would wait until eighth grade before acquiring such social maneuvers. But Felix, from the time he had been old enough to walk and talk, had been tramping around the neighborhood going nowhere and making unintelligible sounds to every adult who tried to converse with him.

Timmy Heidi, who lived at the end of my block, was also going to Bremmer High School. The biggest surprise of eighth grade came on the day that Heidi was announced as the winner of a four-year scholarship to Bremmer. Out of five hundred students who had taken the entrance exam, two hundred, including Heidi, had chosen to take a special scholarship test. Heidi had scored the highest grade.

The nuns at St. Bastion Grammar School were insulted. For eight years, they had given Heidi low grades and told him how stupid he was. After all that, he had the nerve to question their judgment.

If it had been some other student, especially a girl, the nuns would have gone berserk with joy. It would have been the talk of the entire school. Heidi would have been asked to go on a lecture tour to the lower grades so that he could tell the little kids how hard he had to study to achieve it, how proud his parents were of him, and how the nuns had helped him to do so well and all other kinds of garbage.

Heidi's parents were extremely good Catholics. They had eleven children. Their religious fervor had been restrained only by the onset of Mrs. Heidi's menopause.

Heidi once told me that the reason he wanted to go to Bremmer High School was because, at Bremmer, each student got his own locker. Heidi figured that would be as close as he'd ever get to having his own room.

Heidi's father was one of those who thought that if he didn't have a television or radio in the house, people would think he was intelligent. Or maybe it was because, when you have eleven kids, you don't need any more distractions.

During that summer after eighth grade, every time the White Sox played a night game I could expect a phone call from Heidi asking me if I had heard the final score on the television or the radio. By the end of summer, Heidi's father got tired of his using the phone every night; so even that narrow avenue of sports information was denied to Heidi.

It was the night before my first day of high school. I was lying in bed with a layer of Nolsteen Face Cream smeared across my face, listening to the White Sox game on the radio, when I heard a large billowing voice, with nonhuman qualities, bellow outside my window: "Hey, Ryan, are you listening to the White Sox game?"

I got out of bed, limped over to the window (I still had a cast on one of my legs), and tried to pull up the window screen. But it kept sticking along its ridges. After about five tugs, I finally got the window screen high enough to slide smoothly.

Poking my head out. It was a perfect summer night. Two-blankets cool with a star-riddled sky. But I could see nothing. My window, which was on the second floor of the house, opened directly above the driveway of our neighbor, LeRoy Vanson. LeRoy owned a meat truck that he always parked overnight in the driveway. Now all I could hear was the quiet hum of the refrigerator engine on LeRoy's truck.

Being Catholic, I had always been aware of the possibility of miracles. And, like most Catholics, I constantly held out the vague hope that one would happen to me. Once you're involved in a miracle, you're a sure bet for Heaven. That night, staring out the window, I hoped, for but a small second, that just maybe I had been chosen.

That's who was talking to me: God. He was going to chitchat a little about the White Sox's chances for a pennant and then get into the business end of why he had come to see me.

"Eddie, I want you to build a shrine here in LeRoy's driveway in honor of me. After you move the meat truck, of course."

The night air crackled with static. Somewhere in the black, the big voice boomed again. "Hey, Ryan, are you dead or alive?" I was almost sure then that it couldn't be God. Who would know better if I was dead or alive?

Unlike the first coming, when they were caught unaware, this time my ears were tuned for the voice. Something quite familiar was detected. If it was God, He sounded a lot like Timmy Heidi.

Motionless, I continued to hang out the window. A few silent minutes passed. I was ready to pull the window screen down and go back to bed when I again heard the unknown speaker clear its voice of static, readying itself to deliver what was to be its last message. The words were spoken very matter-of-factly but, nevertheless, left no doubt that they were not a case of divine intervention. "Hey, asshole, can you hear me over there?"

The next morning, Timmy Heidi was at my door. We had made previous plans to travel the two miles to Bremmer High School together.

"Why didn't you answer me last night?" he asked.

"I wasn't sure it was you. How did you make your voice so loud?"

"One of those battery-operated megaphones. My father's using it on the job he's working now, when he has to talk to guys who are three or four floors above him."

"Hey, that's neat," I said.

"Yeah," Heidi agreed weakly, "but I got something that'll work better." He leaned down, reached into the school bag at his feet, and pulled out a pile of wire and two plastic microphones that were entangled in the mess. "I got it for Christmas this year. I strung it up a couple of times between my house and the garage and it works great."

"So what do you wanna do with it now?"

"When the White Sox play a game," Heidi began, "there's no way for me to find out the score till the next morning. There's no television or radio in the house, I ain't allowed to use the telephone anymore, and if I use that megaphone again my old man says he'll poke my eyes out."

"Did he really say he'd poke your eyes out?"

"Something like that. Anyway, I figure I can string this walkie-talkie between our two houses and then I'll be able to call you to get the scores."

"That's crazy," I said, "we live more than a half a block apart. It'll never stretch that far. Besides, we've got to get to school. We don't want to be late on our first day."

"Maybe it will," said Heidi. "We can try it. It won't take long. If it doesn't work, it doesn't work. You go up to your bedroom, Ryan, and open the window. I'll toss you one of the mikes and then I'll start stringing it out."

I went upstairs, opened the window, and pulled up the screen, which again kept sticking along its ridges. Heidi was already standing below, untangling the wires of the walkie-talkie. In a few minutes he had the walkie-talkie reduced to a group of neat coils looped around various pickets of the fence, which ran alongside my backyard and continued along the edge of the property between my house and LeRoy's driveway. Heidi put one of the microphones in his hand and then carefully unwound the first coil from the fence picket. He looked up at the window.

"Are you ready, Ryan?"

"Ready."

Heidi dropped the coil of wire at his feet and tossed the microphone up in the direction of my window. It floated lightly toward me, paused briefly, and then proceeded to skim a few bricks on its way back down to Heidi.

"You didn't throw it high enough," I yelled.

"Honest to God?" Heidi said in mock shock. "Look, Ryan, it's not gonna hit you in the head. You gotta stretch for it."

"I'm not gonna fall out of the window for the damn thing."

"Just catch it."

"All right, all right."

Three more attempts fell short. A fourth attempt sailed right by the window but I missed it.

"Wait a minute, Ryan," said Heidi, "we're not getting

anywhere this way. Look, I'm gonna get up on the fence and stretch out my arm toward the window. Now if you stretch out, there'll only be a few feet between us. I can just flip it to you."

It worked perfectly, to a point. I easily caught the microphone. But as Heidi jumped off the fence, his feet fell on the wire, which was now running up to my bedroom window.

At that precise moment I was standing just inside the window, taking a close look at the microphone. It had two little buttons on it, a red one and a black one. I pushed its red button.

The microphone responded immediately as it attempted to yank me out the window. The side of my head slammed into the window, then quickly slid under and past it. I was about a third of the way out the window when my mind blitzed to the conclusion that if I dropped the microphone, I might very well save my life.

Sinking against the wall beneath the window. Never again would I push a red button. The side of my head felt as if someone had tried to jam a watermelon through my ear. My heart was beating somewhere beneath my navel.

As I sat there, I could hear new pimples popping up all over my forehead from the streams of sweat that were careening across my face. I began feeling the weight of the dandruff as it multiplied itself on top of my head. Both armpits were pumping out sweat. Under the cast, the skin started itching like mad from the puddles of perspiration now floating over it. On the other leg, the knee was swollen with pain. I had smashed it against the wall when I had almost gone out the window.

I tried calling out to Heidi, but all my voice could produce was a barely audible squeak followed by a moan four octaves lower in tone, which sounded as if it had come from my toes.

The ears slowly became conscious of a stereophonic nagging. Below the window, Heidi was hollering at me for throwing the microphone at him, while my mother was yelling up the stairs.

"Eddie. Eddie, are you ready for your first day of high school?"

In front of Bremmer High School, on a large marble stand, was a bronze statue of St. Patrick Bremmer with outstretched arms. St. Patrick Bremmer was the founder of the religious order that taught at Bremmer High School.

On the marble stand were some words written in Latin, which supposedly said something about Catholic education being the best way to turn a fine young Catholic boy into a fine young Catholic man. Timmy Heidi claimed that the English translation was "Welcome, Suckers."

Directly behind Bremmer High School was its huge "athletic field." The athletic equipment consisted of grass.

According to the Bremmer High School Handbook, all the rules and regulations of the school were aimed at contributing to the growth of the fine young Catholic boy as he entered fine young Catholic manhood. Students therefore were not allowed to wear black leather jackets, have dirt under their fingernails, go up stairs that were marked "down" or down stairs that were marked "up," chew gum, hitchhike in the vicinity of the school, or wear cleats on their shoes, tattoos on their skin, or hair on their faces.

The hair on a student's head had to be worn in one of two basic styles, the "Crewcut" or the "Regular." A "Regular" haircut was an old Crewcut with a part in it that could barely be combed sideways. Any student who wore his hair in a "Detroit," "Ducktail," or any other "long" hair style was subject to suspension or expulsion.

In the history of Bremmer High School there had even been a few cases of a faculty member actually escorting a long-haired student to the local barber. Inevitably, the faculty member involved was bald.

The Bremmer High School Handbook also stated the dress code that was to be observed. All students were required to wear a sport coat, a tie, and a belt. The belt was considered necessary wearing apparel because many students showed up at school looking like they had spent the night in a wind tunnel. With the belt requirement, the administration reasoned that the students would at least look neat around the waist.

During every school year, some kid who wasn't planning on staying at Bremmer High School anyway would talk about coming to school with nothing on but a sport coat, a tie, and a belt.

Most students wore the same sport coats for all four years. You could tell how much growing a senior had done since he had been in high school by how his sport coat fit him. Some seniors had done so well in the growing department that they looked like they were wearing short-sleeve sport coats.

On their last day of school, the seniors would hold their traditional bonfire in the middle of the athletic field. They'd throw in their school books, papers, perhaps a few underclassmen who had annoyed them, but, most particularly, their sport coats. Many of the sport coats, however, looked about the same coming out of the bonfire as they did going in.

The record for the continual wearing of one sport coat at Bremmer High School—sixteen years—was in the process of being set while I was a freshman. The fourth of the four Fennigan brothers, Ronnie Fennigan, was still using the same sport coat that all three of his older brothers had worn at Bremmer.

On an autumn afternoon that had unexpectedly turned cool, Ronnie Fennigan made the mistake of wearing the family sport coat home rather than leaving it in his locker, which was the usual thing to do. Before Ronnie Fennigan arrived home, an old lady offered to give him money, a bus driver closed the door in his face, a cop threatened to arrest him for vagrancy, two dogs bit him, and a weirdo tried to pick him up.

Although students didn't do much growing up at Bremmer High School, they certainly did a lot of growing older. You would see a freshman with the body of a bookmark, wearing glasses so big that his face looked like the front of a bus, walking down the hall and asking someone where the second floor was. Sharing the hall with him might be a senior who looked as if he had borrowed his arms from Smokey the Bear.

Bremmer High School was owned, operated, and mostly staffed by the Brothers of the St. Bremmer Religious Order. The school also employed a number of lay teachers.

In the Catholic Church, religious brothers are the male equivalent of nuns. Brothers cannot say Mass, hear confessions, or perform any priestly functions. Most orders of brothers devote themselves to some particular social function, usually teaching. There are orders of brothers, however, as there are orders of nuns, that specialize in such activities as hospital work, social work, or simply in working regular jobs among the people and helping out where they can.

It was not uncommon at Bremmer High School to encounter a brother who liked to give the impression that he was a direct descendant of Attila the Hun and that he'd kick the shit out of you if you looked in the wrong direction.

Many of the students also seemed to enjoy embellishing the folklore of brutality that surrounded different brothers. Sophomores spent a fair amount of their free time terrifying freshmen with tales of various brothers' hitting histories. "You got Brother Gruppi? Oh, man, he's the worst. He's got this huge leather strap and when he gets going, you can hear that thing all over the school." "Whatever you do, don't talk in Brother Courtdown's class. If he gets pissed off at you, he'll punch you right in the face. He damn near broke some kid's nose last year."

In temperament and personality, however, the majority of the brothers were more like Julie Andrews than Attila. There were a few brothers who were truly tough, but not many.

Brother Well loved to give the impression that he was mean and rotten. The narrowed eyes stared straight down his nose at you. His hands, even when resting at his side, were clenched into fists. He wore his lips as if they had just tasted sandpaper. Even his crewcut looked angry. Brother Well, as did many of the other brothers, really acted like a tough guy. Therein lay the danger. With Brother Well, it wasn't all acting.

Brother Well had been an amateur boxer before joining the brothers. Just because he had put on a black cassock, Brother Well saw no reason why he should have to give up his hobby.

His first teaching assignment was in Engleton Catholic High School on the North Side of Chicago. A week after he began teaching, Brother Well got his first opportunity to demonstrate his skills. Two senior football players in his class decided to challenge his authority by goofing around. Brother Well gave both of them a warning, which they ignored. He then gave each of them a punch, which they did not ignore.

One of the football players' mothers was the head of the Engleton High School Mothers Club. At the time, the mothers club was in the midst of raising funds for a new wing to the library. The football player's mother demanded that the principal transfer Brother Well to another school. A new wing for the library or Brother Well. Hardly a difficult choice. A week later Brother Well was at Bremmer High School.

During the five years that Brother Well had been at Bremmer, he had not found it necessary to maim any student. During those years no student had ever said more than two words to Brother Well. Those two words were "Yes, Brother."

Percentage grades, rather than letter grades, were given at Bremmer. A failing grade was anything below seventy percent. If in the final quarter of the school year you received a failing grade in a major course, then you had to go to summer school for ten weeks to make up the course.

It was traditional that, no matter how rotten a student did in a class, the lowest grade a teacher would give him on the report card would be forty percent. Why such courtesy, I don't know. Maybe it was because, even with a forty percent in one course, a student still had a slim chance of getting a decent overall average if he did extremely well in his other courses.

The only one who did not give out "gentleman 40s" was Brother Well. He gave you exactly what you earned. In Brother Well's class you lost credit for not doing your homework, which enabled some kid to come out with a final grade of minus twelve percent.

Once, some student went to Brother Well to complain about a failing grade. The words that Brother Well said to him were never before, nor ever again, spoken by a teacher to a student. "I flunked you. You didn't flunk yourself."

One good thing could be said about Brother Well. There wasn't a member of the faculty who could stand him.

The makeup of the lay faculty was pretty much the same as that of the brothers; a few savages, a few nuts, some nice guys, and a lot of guys who weren't anything in particular.

There were four different course programs to which a student could be assigned at Bremmer: The Honors Program, Engineering, Academic, and the Business Program.

The Honors Program contained the guys who had scored in the 99.999th percentile on their high school entrance examinations, worked out calculus problems for their own amusement during lunch time, had asked Santa Claus for a chemistry set instead of a bicycle, and never did notice when weekends or puberty came around.

Not all of them were that way though. Timmy Heidi went into the Honors Program and he certainly knew when weekends came around. His problem was that he couldn't tell when they ended.

Besides Heidi, the only other Honors kid that I knew fairly well was Bernie Gaggin, who sat across the table from me in the cafeteria during my sophomore year. You knew he was an Honors kid because when somebody dropped a tray, he was the only one at the table who didn't stand up and applaud.

Bernie Gaggin was extremely bright. He could read upside down. If I was reading the school newspaper or something and he wanted to read it too, he'd ask me to put it in the middle of the table. He'd then read it upside down as fast as I'd read it right side up.

When it came to getting grades, Bernie Gaggin was a real hustler. He was always bringing something to the lunch table that he had either already used that morning or was going to use that afternoon for a classroom demonstration. One day it would be plants for a Biology class. On another day it might be some magazine articles for an English class.

Teachers love that kind of stuff and Bernie Gaggin knew it. I suppose the reason teachers are so impressed by it is that it shows the student has thought about the crummy class somewhere besides in it.

Five years after he graduated from Bremmer, Bernie Gaggin was arrested for exposing himself in a supermarket parking lot. The unavoidable consequence of being too good at "show and tell."

The Honors kids supposedly took the most difficult

courses from the toughest teachers. But according to Timmy Heidi, that's not the way things worked out. He claimed that the teachers who taught the Honors kids knew, of course, that they were Honors kids and graded them with that in mind. Very rarely, said Timmy Heidi, was an Honors kid ever given anything less than a ninety percent, not because he never earned anything less than that but because, being an Honors kid, he didn't deserve anything less.

The Engineering Program was filled with guys who were theoretically second in intelligence only to the Honors group. In fact, the Engineering Program was about the same as the Academic Program, except that in the Engineering Program sutdents were required to take a number of shop courses. Tom Lanner went into the Engineering Program.

Felix Lindor and I were enrolled in the Academic Program, which was for the "average" student. In the Bremmer High School catalog it was stated that the Academic Program was designed to prepare the student for college. The label "Academic" was a phony. What course program isn't "academic"? Besides, both the Honors Program and the Engineering Program were also obviously geared for the college-bound student. An accurate title for the Academic Program would have been something like "The Lazy as Sin but if They Break Their Asses They Might Get into College" Program. Such a title, however, would have been too long for the forms that had to be filled out at the beginning of each year.

The basic difference between the Academic and the Engineering students, besides the fact that the Engineering students weren't quite as lazy, was that the Academic students were derelicts when it came to anything mechanical. Requiring Academic students to take shop courses would have been genocide. We didn't have enough limbs to get through even one week of working around moving machinery.

Tom Lanner was a typical Engineering student. Whenever we saw something mechanical in operation, he would react by making the comment that, I suspect, most Engineering students would have made under similar circumstances. "I wonder how it works?" And I would always follow up his observation with the one that all Academic students shared: "Who cares?"

Then there was the Business Program, which was for the dull normal, though most of the guys who were in it were neither. The Business Program taught its participants little more than the multiplication tables and oral reading. Most of the students in Business supposedly had I.Q.s that sounded like basement apartment numbers. If a Business student wanted to sign up for the course in typing, he had to first take a prerequisite course that introduced him to the alphabet. For pursuing such academic endeavors, the students in the Business Program became known throughout Bremmer High School as the "Jolly Numbers Boys." A Jolly Numbers boy was the kind of kid who, from kindergarten on, could never keep his coloring inside the lines, and could care less.

On my first day at Bremmer High School, we incoming freshmen spent the morning filling out the usual forty-seven thousand forms. "Last name first, first name, and middle initial last," that every institution demands before it will allow you to be eaten up by it. In the afternoon the entire student body was herded into the gym, which doubled as the school auditorium, to hear Brother Purity, the principal of Bremmer High School, speak.

Although in his late forties, Brother Purity sported a suit of skin that was completely wrinkle-free. Thick blond hair, neatly combed with a straight part, covered the top of his head. Brother Purity also had sparkling white teeth, rosy cheeks, clear blue eyes, and such perfect little ears that it was obvious they had never even heard a dirty word. His mother never had to take baby pictures. All she had to do was look at her son. He hadn't changed at all since the day he turned two.

The seniors sat on the main floor of the gym on folding chairs while the underclassmen, depending on what year they were in, sat in various sections of the foldaway bleachers. Brother Purity spoke with a Boston accent although he had never been farther east than Cleveland. Most of his words were directed at us freshmen.

The first thing that Brother Purity said in welcoming us to Bremmer High School was that we would be amazed at how fast our four years of high school would go by. That's what they all say.

When I was in first grade, my nun told our class that we should "enjoy" our grammar school years because, in no time at all, the years would be gone. No time at all! The reason I don't fear Hell today is because I know that eternity can't be as long as the eight years I spent in grammar school.

When my mother dragged the family to Indiana for a three-week vacation, she told me to quit complaining because the time would pass quickly. During the 30,240 minutes I spent there, I discovered that absolutely nothing, least of all time, passes quickly in Indiana.

I bet if I murdered somebody and got a 199-year

prison sentence, the first thing the warden would say to me would be, "You're going to be amazed at how fast the 199 years go by."

Brother Purity then spent the next hour talking about the greatest bullshit topic of all, school spirit. He said that we should love our school, respect it, and care about it. I thought at one point he was going to say "caress it," but he didn't. Brother Purity chimed out about how we shouldn't just come to school every day, attend classes, and then go home. We should, instead, take an active interest in Bremmer High School because it took an active interest in us. We should participate in the school's athletic programs, get involved in its numerous academic and social clubs, and join such organizations as the school newspaper and yearbook staffs.

My eyes remained fastened on the figure of Brother Purity as he sprayed his furious frenzy of faith in Bremmer High School. Hoarsely, he concluded his speech. "Freshmen," he said, "it's up to you."

Almost all the freshmen stood up and applauded like mad. I noticed that even a few of the sophomores were standing. But not a junior or senior budged. Nor did Felix Lindor, who was sitting next to me. I was clapping so hard my hands were stinging. I looked down at Felix. He was deeply involved in studying his fingernails.

But I had bought it. Brother Purity's message had somehow managed to slip through that shell of cynicism that had, in the past few years, begun to grow around my brain.

The nice part about starting high school was that, in a way, it was a chance to start my life over again. All the dumb things that I had ever done were now locked away in that world of grammar school. The failed tests, the unfinished homework, lost workbooks, and the embarrassing moments of getting slugged by the nuns had all fallen, on the day that I had graduated from grammar school, into an era that no longer existed.

Now, I decided, was the time to get myself out of that mold of mediocrity that I had, up to this age, poured my life into. As we marched out of the gym that Friday afternoon, I made up my mind that I was going to get fantastic grades for all four years, earn a varsity letter in at least ten different sports, and join forty-seven extracurricular activities and become president of all of them. No doubt, I reasoned, when I graduated Bremmer High School would retire my locker number.

By Monday morning, however, I had pretty well sobered up from Brother Purity's words. I was proud of myself for recovering so quickly from such a heavy snow job. It was a sure sign that I was, at last, outgrowing a childhood affliction I had suffered with four years: an overactive gullibility gland.

When I was a kid, it usually took me weeks to discover that reality wasn't nearly as exciting as the rhetoric some people used to describe it.

In the third grade, a missionary priest came to the classroom and delivered a forty-minute monologue about how we should give money to the missions so that our class could buy pagan babies, who were somewhere in Africa, and turn them into Christians.

The missionary never really told us who was selling the pagan babies, but he made it very clear how much each pagan baby cost. Five dollars.

He even gave our nun forms to fill out for each pagan baby that we bought. On the form there was a space for the name of the pagan baby. For some reason, all of

38

these babies were nameless, so whoever paid the five bucks got to name one.

I was so excited about the whole thing that instead of just chipping in with the rest of the class, I went out and, in less than a month, earned five dollars so that I could buy my own pagan baby.

During his talk the missionary said that when we gave our money to the missions, we would feel the thrill of God's love. By the time I had earned the five bucks, my enthusiasm was waning. When I dropped it into the mission can, I can honestly say that I did not feel the thrill of God's love, at least not five dollars' worth.

I told the nun I wanted to name my pagan baby "Trigger" after Roy Rogers' horse. I thought that would have been a neat name for a kid. It sounded both mean and cool. I wouldn't have minded having a name like that. The nun didn't go for it though. She put "Francis" down on the form.

That night I dreamed that the pagan baby grew up, came to America, and hunted me down for naming him "Francis." He cornered me in an alley and put a gun to my head. I started yelling, "No, I wanted to name you Trigger . . ."—which was when he blew my head off.

I did, nevertheless, spend a few days of my first week of high school checking out some of the extracurricular activities that Bremmer offered. I thought about trying out for the freshman football team. But after looking in the mirror at my 115-pound frame, I decided not to, because of my religious beliefs. Catholics aren't allowed to commit suicide.

Most of the extracurricular groups didn't seem anxious to take on new members. The one organization that did seem interested in my possible membership was the "Sodality of Our Lady," which was the Salvation Army of Bremmer High School.

Its members went around collecting food for poor people, taught catechism to the Catholic kids who lived in the ghettos, and spent their Saturdays visiting old-age homes. The "Sodality of Our Lady" felt that I would be a welcome addition to their organization. Both members wanted me to join.

I don't remember much about the first six or seven months of my high school years mainly because I didn't do anything worth remembering, which became apparent as my freshman year tumbled into the months of spring. By then I was doing one great of job of blowing my grades.

I was required to take five major subjects and two minor subjects. My major subjects were English, Religion, General Science, Latin, and Algebra. The two minor subjects were Art and Music Appreciation.

Flunking a major subject was serious business. It meant ten weeks of summer school. But the minor subjects were nothing to worry about. Nobody ever flunked them. As long as a guy made a minimum amount of effort, he was given a passing grade.

In Art a "minimum amount of effort" was being able to identify the basic colors. Even that wasn't always necessary. Gerald Stopsen passed Art and he was totally colorblind.

In Music Appreciation we spent most of our time listening to classical music. I don't know why. At that time my appreciation of music extended to the point that I got goose pimples when I heard the "Star-Spangled Banner."

It was almost impossible to stay awake during a Music

Appreciation class. The moment you walked into the room, your eyelids gained twenty pounds apiece and your head kept wanting to fall off your neck. Brother Roon, the music teacher, took it as a personal insult whenever a student fell asleep in class. He was a man who lived in a constant state of insult. Brother Roon used his grading power to appease his hurt feelings. Only devout insomniacs did well in Music Appreciation.

In three of my major subjects, English, Religion, and General Science, I was managing to get by. I've always enjoyed English, as much as I could enjoy anything that was taught in school. Besides, I've always had the ability to write a five-page report on a book after reading nothing more than its title. Religion was another "unflunkable" subject at Bremmer. About the only way you could do it would be to come right out and claim that you hated God's guts. Even then, if you gave a good reason for your hate, say because He allows poverty in the world or some other asinine reason, you'd still pass. My General Science teacher, Mr. Luce, didn't have time to fail anybody. He was too busy having a nervous breakdown, courtesy of Ernie Kogan and some Jolly Numbers boys.

Mr. Luce taught four sections of General Science a day. One of those sections was comprised of Jolly Numbers boys, among them Ernie Kogan, who were required to take General Science in their junior year.

Ernie Kogan was one of those glorious creations of God, an "athlete"; more specifically, a football player. Ernie's father had seen to that. A week after Ernie was born, when his mother brought him home from the hospital, Ernie's father made Ernie kick a thirty-yard field goal before he'd allow him in the house.

41

Ernie was eight years old before he discovered that pillows were soft. For some reason, that night he had gone to bed without his football helmet on.

When Ernie Kogan was in grammar school, part of his training each morning consisted of opening the overhead garage doors for his father. Ernie would get a running start from the back of the garage and then bounce the overhead doors up out of the way with a perfectly executed shoulder block.

I shared an English class with Ernie Kogan. One morning Ernie admitted to the teacher that he didn't understand a Shakespearean play that had been assigned for homework.

"Ernie," said our English teacher, "in order to understand it, you've got to read it slowly."

Replied Ernie, "That's the only way I read."

Ernie Kogan played center on the Bremmer football team. The job of the center is not too intellectually demanding. All he does is snap the ball to the quarterback and then try to knock down anybody who goes by. Ernie had the perfect build for the position. He looked like a ten-foot brick with a head on it.

By his junior year Ernie Kogan's football fetishism was beginning to take its toll on his body. Ernie's right shoulder had developed a twitch. On the days that he had it, about every thirty seconds his right shoulder would flinch up and giggle.

One shoulder giggling was hardly a threat to Mr. Luce's mental stability. The problem was that Ernie Kogan, since he was a center, liked to see things up close so he always sat in the front row. His fellow classmates, being Jolly Numbers boys, were quick to lap up any chance for a laugh. They decided that whenever Ernie flinched, they would all flinch. Ernie, of course, didn't know what was going on. If he had, he would have dismantled at least one of the mockers just to teach the others a lesson.

After a few months the routine began to wear on Mr. Luce. Every time Ernie Kogan flinched, two seconds later, in perfect sync, the thirty-nine guys behind him would flinch. Another two seconds and Mr. Luce would flinch.

After the football season Ernie Kogan's flinch became much less noticeable. The rest of the Jolly Numbers boys had tired of mocking it, anyway, and were looking for new ways to amuse themselves. By the end of the school year the only one still flinching was Mr. Luce.

Although I was barely staying alive in English, Religion, and General Science, the body was quickly growing cold in Algebra and Latin.

Mr. Wendell, my algebra teacher, was a very nice guy who looked exactly like an algebra teacher should look. He wore his hair in a stick-straight crewcut, never allowed himself to be seen without a bow tie, and had a nose that met you at the door. Years later I would overhear Mr. Wendell tell someone that the reason he always wore a bow tie was so that students would talk about it and not him.

On more than one occasion, Mr. Wendell had just as much as said that teaching Algebra was the most thrilling way a man could spend his life. When he told his wife he loved her, Mr. Wendell probably put it in an equation.

During one of his classes Mr. Wendell informed us that he and some of his neighbors had put up a garage the previous Sunday afternoon. His eyes glowed behind the thick glasses as he told us that because of his knowledge of algebraic formulas, he was the only one who knew how to construct the corners of the foundation.

I thought it was a very depressing story, to hear about someone who devoted all those years to a subject that allowed him to be a big shot for only one Sunday afternoon.

Although I was doing extremely lousy in Algebra, I still liked Mr. Wendell and he apparently did not find me too hard to take either. Such was not the case in my Latin class.

Unless you plan on becoming a priest, there is no reason in the world to learn Latin. Not only is the language dead, but so are most of the people who teach it. Brother Coratelli, my Latin teacher, was no exception.

Brother Coratelli was so old it was a strong possibility that Latin was his native tongue. Most of the time he was sleepy. Like everybody else, Brother Coratelli found it difficult to stay awake in his presence.

He was also a slob. There were quite a few other teachers at Bremmer, among both the laymen and the religious, who fell into that category, but none fell nearly as deep as Brother Coratelli. If he got a chalk mark on his cassock in September, it would still be there in May. On those rare occasions when Brother Coratelli walked down into the rows of students, kids on either side of him would slide to the far side of their seats in an attempt to avoid the silent sea of smell that rolled in a few feet ahead of his approach. No matter what the temperature was outside, windows remained opened. Brother Coratelli was nicknamed among the students as "Sort-a-Smelli."

On the first day of class Brother Coratelli tried to justify the existence of a Latin course. He told us that through the study of Latin we would greatly increase our English vocabulary, since many English words are derived from Latin.

Like a real ass I raised my hand and asked Brother Coratelli why, if such were the case, wouldn't it be a lot simpler to just study the English dictionary and forget the Latin altogether. Why I did something that obnoxious, I'll never know. Maybe the pimples were beginning to affect my brain. Brother Coratelli mumbled something about me not having any idea of what I was talking about and instructed the class to open their books to Lesson Number One. From that day on, he hated my guts.

After that little episode Brother Coratelli certainly had sufficient reason. That was a very dumb thing I did that day. We all have those moments, I guess. We look back upon them a few weeks later, or months or even years later, and, alone with our thoughts, we cringe with embarrassment, unable to believe that we could really make that big of a jerk out of ourselves. The trouble with me is, shortly after I think like this I do something that later becomes new "cringe" material.

Being a teacher, Brother Coratelli couldn't come right out and state that he hated my guts, so he said it in the same way that all teachers say it to students: "I don't like your attitude."

Teachers are great ones for saying one thing and meaning another. For instance, when they say "I'm disappointed in you," they really mean "Just what I expected." The Bremmer High School teachers did their best double-talking at the parent-teacher conferences.

My mother would come home from one of those and she'd tell me that one of my teachers said that I "didn't apply" myself. In other words, I never did a thing. Or some teacher would tell her that I lacked "self-motivation," which basically meant that I never wanted to do anything. My parents were always being told that I wasn't "academically oriented," a polite way of saying that I had no business being in school.

A teacher would become so accustomed to double-talking with parents that he would forget how to talk straight to a student. Mr. Wendell, my algebra teacher, must have asked me a hundred times why I was such a poor student. Being a freshman, I didn't understand what he was saying. Poor student? What was he talking about? I had some money in my pocket. I just didn't comprehend what the man was really asking me: "Why are you such a goddamn dummy?"

Brother Coratelli didn't say "I don't like your attitude" to me very often. When you hate a person's guts, you usually try to avoid talking to him altogether. But occasionally Brother Coratelli's blob-brown eyes would be lazily drifting across the horizons of his half-closed eyelids when they would bump into the image of me sitting motionless at my desk.

Mankind was supposedly evolved from the apes. That may be true, but somewhere in my ancient family tree, way up the line, one of the apes must have played around with a rabbit. If a rabbit's in trouble it remains totally still, hoping to God that no one even notices it's there.

In a class where I had no desire to be called on, I took the rabbit approach to survival. I'd sit there as still as a statue, my eyes staring blankly into whatever paper or book was on top of my desk.

If a rabbit is spotted it runs like hell. I, on the other hand, stood my ground. If, despite my immobility, a teacher noticed me and called on me to recite, I'd stand up and fake it as best I could. Standing up instead of running must have been the ape influence in me. Rabbits are a lot smarter than apes.

Brother Coratelli would call on me. I'd stand. He'd ask a question. I'd either give him the wrong answer or admit that I didn't know the answer. Then his saggy head would shake while his mouth would "tsk-tsk" all over the place. Occasionally Brother Coratelli would follow up this ritual with the comment "Mr. Ryan, I don't like your attitude," i.e. I hate your guts.

One day when Brother Coratelli said that with slightly less disdain than he normally did, I took the chance of asking him what he meant, even though I already knew. I asked him very meekly, my words slowly sliding forward as if they were the thread aiming for the eye of the needle. I didn't want to give Brother Coratelli the impression that I was challenging his authority. Standing up to a brother's authority was an excellent way of getting into big trouble.

"What do I mean, Mr. Ryan?" Brother Coratelli mumbled. He was getting so mad at me, he was almost awake. "I mean what I say, I don't like your attitude."

"I know that, Brother," I commented quietly. "I just wondered exactly what you meant by that."

"I don't like the way you come to this class. Is that clear enough for you, Mr. Ryan?"

"Yes, Brother."

It was very clear. When Brother Coratelli said he

didn't like the way I showed up for class, he was just using different words to say he would have been much happier if I didn't show up at all for class, which was to say he couldn't stand the sight of me. In other words, he hated my guts.

Latin, like any foreign language, is one of the worst subjects that a lousy student can take. In order to do well in Latin, you've got to study every night. Unlike other subjects, where you can cram the night before an examination and sometimes scrape through to a passing grade, Latin demands consistent study habits. Inconsistent study habits, however, are the true mark of a lousy student. I myself, being an exceptionally lousy student, would follow up a night of hard study with six or seven weeks of academic abstinence.

As the weeks of freshman year rolled into months, I became increasingly terrified of being called on by Brother Coratelli. It's one thing for a teacher to call on you and realize that you don't know what he taught you yesterday. It's quite another for him to discover, through a series of questions, each one going further back into the material, that you have been sitting in his classroom for almost an entire school year and that you don't know *anything at all! Nothing!* Not even the Latin word for "boy."

If I were a teacher I'd find that very depressing. I'd have to wonder how good a teacher I could be if some mope could sit in my class for nine months and not learn a damn thing. I had a feeling, though, that if Brother Coratelli made such a discovery, he would become enraged, not depressed.

Brother Coratelli was aware that I didn't know much Latin because I had easily flunked his midyear exam.

What he didn't realize, I'm sure, was that not only had I not learned a thing since the midyear exam, but I had also managed to forget everything I had learned up to that point.

As I sat through the last month of Latin classes, nothing on me moved but the second hand on my watch.

With only a few weeks to go before the end of freshman year and the final examinations, I was not only going down for the third time in Algebra and Latin but I was also floundering in Music Appreciation, since I had not handed in a "busy work" folder. I wasn't that concerned about passing Music Appreciation. I didn't think they could make me go to summer school for it. What would I do? Go to school for ten weeks during the summer and hum?

Just to make sure, I went to the principal's office and asked the secretary what the policy was about failing a minor subject and having to go to summer school to make it up. The secretary, after entering Brother Purity's office and discussing it with him for a few moments, came out and informed me that there was no policy because no one in the history of the school had ever failed a minor subject.

During the last few weeks before the final exams, I spent every weekday night studying Algebra with a friend of my father's. He really knew the stuff. But there was nothing I could do about Latin. Almost everyone who knew Latin well had been dead for over a thousand years.

We took our final exams in the last week of May. About ten days later, we were told, we would receive our report cards in the mail. Not having handed in the "busy work" folder, I already knew that I had flunked

Music Appreciation. Even though it didn't involve going to summer school, I still felt crummy about it. I was the first, and, as far as I know, the last kid to flunk Music Appreciation at Bremmer High School.

I always had delusions of growing up and running for the United States presidency. Therefore I tried to keep the really rotten or dumb things that I did a secret. But flunking Music Appreciation was now a matter of public record. I could already see a headline of the future: INVESTIGATE REPORT THAT PRESIDENTIAL CANDIDATE EDDIE RYAN IS MUSIC APPRECIATION FLUNKIE.

After taking all the finals, I felt that I had a decent chance of getting through Algebra. Not that I had passed the final examination. I did put enough down, though, to show Mr. Wendell that I wasn't a complete imbecile. More importantly, during the last weeks of the school year I mentioned to him almost daily that I had been working my ass off studying the stuff every week-day night with that friend of my father's. Mr. Wendell knowing that, the odds were heavy against him flunking me.

Amazingly, there was still a possibility of me passing Latin. Brother Coratelli unexplainably made the final a multiple-choice exam. I've always been fairly lucky on those.

During the week that I waited for the report card to come through the mail, I thought often about the upcoming summer. It was to be my fourteenth and probably the last one in which I wouldn't have to work at least part-time. It had all the makings of a great summer. I was now old enough to stay away from the house most of the day and even to get out a few hours at night. I was also allowed to get farther away from the house than ever before. Yet I was still young enough that I didn't have to waste much of my freedom or time on work. I'd get stuck doing some things around the house, cutting the lawn, cleaning the basement, the usual house chores. But that kind of work was no big deal. The rest of the time I'd be able to spend playing baseball, walking around the neighborhood shooting the bull with guys like Heidi, Lanner, and Felix Lindor, calling up girls and maybe even stopping over at their houses, and just plain goofing off.

But flunking Latin would mess up everything. For ten weeks, I'd have to be at Bremmer High School every weekday morning at eight o'clock.

Having to go to summer school would also be a very humiliating experience. My neighbors, who would see me leaving the house every morning at seven o'clock, dressed so neatly that I had to be going to school, would finally have solid evidence for something they had long suspected: I was indeed a loser.

Roger Darby, a kid who lived across the street from me and who had started at Bremmer a year before I did, had flunked a course in his freshman year. Every morning at seven o'clock he would leave his house with a huge sack of rolled newspapers slung over his shoulder. Roger figured he'd fool his neighbors by giving them the impression that he was going out to deliver newspapers. It might have worked except that every morning at eleven o'clock, Roger would return to his house with the same sack of newspapers.

There was no one home but me on that day the report card came in the mail. As the mailman handed me two "occupant" letters, a *Time* magazine, and that envelope

51

with a return address of "Bremmer High School," I tried to think about how much Brother Coratelli, old "Sort-a-Smelli," probably stunk during the hot summer weather. But my nose's imagination couldn't comprehend it.

Ripping open the envelope and pulling out the folded piece of cardboard. My eyes quickly zipped down the column of grade percentages. But not quickly enough. They still saw the forty percent sitting across from the words "Introduction to Latin."

It was a "Sort-a-Smelli" summer.

CATHOLIC GIRLS

Fifteen years old. The beginnings of the stud stage. Daily, that luscious animal urge, the sex drive, was rapidly swelling within me until it began ballooning up against every pore of my body. A walking atom bomb, demanding to be exploded. But I was a Catholic boy in a world of Catholic girls. There was simply no one to drop it on.

The neighborhood that I grew up in on Chicago's South Side was about half Catholic and half "Public." A "Public" was anyone who wasn't Catholic. Since Catholics attended their own schools, had their own scouting troops, social events, and even their own cemeteries, it was hardly surprising that the vast majority of kids in the neighborhood tended to hang around with their own kind. Besides, the nuns constantly told us Catholics that if we hung around with non-Catholic kids, we'd have to set good examples for them. According to the nuns, "more" was expected of Catholic students. So even when an opportunity arose, most of us Catholic kids avoided hanging around with "Publics" just so we wouldn't have to waste our time setting good examples.

But it wasn't until I was a sophomore at Bremmer

High School that I was told, in a religion class, to avoid all members of the opposite sex who happened to be "Public." "If you regularly associate with non-Catholic girls," said Brother Loevinger, "then you run the risk of getting seriously involved with one. Before you realize it, you end up marrying her without fully comprehending the tremendous consequences of what you've done."

The "tremendous consequences" was a "mixed marriage"; in other words, a marriage between a Catholic and a non-Catholic. Theoretically such marriages were forbidden by the Church. Dispensations, however, were fairly easy to obtain. The reasoning of the Church was probably that any Catholic who was rotten enough to even consider marrying a non-Catholic was certainly rotten enough to get married outside the Catholic religion—so the Church might as well give its permission. All the Church asked the non-Catholic to do was to sign away his or her life.

If you were a non-Catholic and you married a Catholic, you had to agree not to interfere with your partner's religious practices, even if you couldn't stand fish and you didn't like getting up early on Sunday morning. Furthermore, you had to sign an agreement that you would raise all the children that resulted from the marriage in the Catholic faith. Catholics, even when they made up only half the team, always "resulted" in a lot of children. Mixed marriages, unlike regular Catholic marriages, were not allowed to be performed within the railings of the altar. Obviously God wasn't in any big rush to get too close to a non-Catholic either.

According to Brother Loevinger, almost all marriages failed anyway and, of the few that succeeded, none of them were mixed marriages.

"Remember, boys," warned Brother Loevinger, "if you never date a non-Catholic girl, you're never going to get yourself involved in a mixed marriage."

Barney Biscel, who was in that class, proved Brother Loevinger wrong. Barney, who always did seem to enjoy gym a little too much, moved out to California three years after he graduated from high school and "married" another homosexual who was, of all things, a non-Catholic. Barney's guardian angel probably found small consolation in the fact that his charge did not have to worry about the delicate problem of birth control.

Catholicism, like most religions, is not in a big rush to see people enjoy life. Years ago most of us prayed to God for everything: good weather, good crops, good health. But not anymore. Today we've pretty well concluded that God doesn't bother Himself with such trivia as personally looking after the weather. We realize now that good crops depend more on chemicals and soil than on bended knees. When most of us get sick, we much prefer going to the nearest M.D. rather than the closest church.

But these were minor victories of reason over religion, for religion still holds the high card. It always has and it always will. Death.

The only thing we positively know about death is that we're all going to become participants in it, most of us unwillingly. Since there's no way that we can understand what death is all about, we turn to religion so that we might believe what it's all about.

The problem is, however, that most of us don't worry about anything as long as it's at a distance from us. This would be bad news for religion if it didn't try to change the situation. How far can any organization go if all its members are on their deathbeds? So as soon as we're old enough to look into a mirror, religion starts reminding us of death and never lets up until the day we experience it firsthand.

Now if everyone is busy enjoying life, the job of religion is that much tougher. Religion offers us hope where there is none, in death. But most individuals who are shopping around for hope are depressed about the way things presently are. People who are constantly having a good time make lousy Christians.

As everybody knows, including the Catholic Church, one of the best ways of having a good time is sex. So throughout the Church's history it has spent a large amount of its energy going around giving sex a bad name. Even Christ, the first Catholic, apparently didn't have much use for it. Of all the people ever born on this earth, only one has insisted that his mother be a virgin. Christ spent most of his time hanging around with twelve other guys.

The Catholic Church realized that it would have to tolerate some sex among its members. If it didn't, the Church would very shortly have no members at all. So the Church decided to allow its members to have sex, but only under the most painful of circumstances—marriage and children.

The Church had such a hatred for sex that it refused to even mention the name. If you thought about doing it, then it was called an "impure thought." If you went ahead and did it, it was referred to as an "impure act," and "prurient interest," or an "illicit activity." If you did it with your wife, it was the "Marriage Act" or "the privileges of marriage." If you thought about doing it with your neighbor's wife, then it was called "coveting thy neighbor's wife." If you did it with your neighbor's wife, then it was "adultery." If you did it alone, it was "self-abuse." And if you didn't do it at all, it was called "holiness."

Because the Catholic Church was strongly against sex, it also had an extremely negative attitude toward the sexiest thing around—woman. The Church never really forgave Eve for giving that apple to Adam. Women have been under suspicion ever since.

Women aren't allowed to be priests, where all the real power is. Until recently women weren't even allowed to stand inside the altar railing unless they were directly involved in receiving a sacrament. That's why there was no such thing as an "altar girl." In a Catholic wedding ceremony the groom is always served Holy Communion first because he is considered the "head" of the family. The woman is given the consolation prize of being the "heart" of the family. Big deal.

In a final attempt to make sex totally unfun, the Church hierarchy decided that it would convince everyone that sex was just a big bore. But the members of the hierarchy—all of whom were men, naturally—knew, of course, that sex was indeed a lot of laughs. Exactly how they knew I don't know, but they knew. (The Church defines this inherent male knowledge of the pleasure of sex as "passion." Women become passionate only when they start acting "unladylike.") So the Catholic Church, which never had a high opinion of women anyway, aimed this psychological warfare directly at all the Catholic females. Sure enough, it worked.

During my grammar school years the girls, like the boys weren't told anything about sex, except for a talk that was given by one of the parish priests to our eighth grade class. He talked to the boys separately and then to the girls. All he told us boys was that our bodies were temples of the Holy Ghost, that within a very short time some beautiful changes were going to occur to our bodies, and that we should never touch our private parts.

Felix the Filth Fiend Lindor was the only kid who had enough nerve to ask a question. He wanted to know how our parts could be private if everyone knew we had them.

The priest talked to us boys for a half hour. But his speech to the girls lasted less than fifteen minutes. He couldn't have wanted to tell them very much. If he had, his talk would have been closer to fifteen days. Catholic girls would be quicker to understand an explanation of the Blessed Trinity than they would sexual information.

It wasn't until high school that the girls got barraged with purity propaganda. Since almost all the Catholic high schools in Chicago were exclusively for one sex or the other, the nuns, with an all-girl audience and no boys around to cause trouble by presenting the other side, could really get down to serious antisensual business.

Girls were repeatedly admonished by the nuns to dress "modestly"; that is, like nuns. A Catholic girl was supposed to wear her clothes in such a way that all physical signs of her sex were completely concealed. A nun considered a blouse "tight" if it even hinted that there were breasts beneath it. Clothing that concealed as much skin as possible, such as blouses with long sleeves and especially skirts and dresses with low hemlines, was strongly encouraged. In every Catholic girls' school there was at least one nun who spent most of her time running around measuring the distance between the students' hemlines and the floor. The less the distance, the more modest was the girl who was wearing the dress or skirt. A perfectly logical dress code for someone whose own hemline was located three feet beyond her shoes.

Catholic girls were also warned not to wear black patent leather shoes or to allow their dates to take them to places that had white tablecloths. A girl was not to wear black patent leather shoes because, supposedly, such shoes reflected up. The nuns believed that a boy could see up a girl's dress by looking into her black patent leather shoes. White tablecloths were to be avoided because, according to the nuns, they reminded boys of bed.

In fact, the nuns gave boys credit for having far dirtier minds than the boys actually had. I never knew any guy who obtained sexual gratification from black patent shoes, with the possible exception of Felix the Filth Fiend Lindor, who got sexual gratification from everything. White tablecloths didn't remind me, or anyone else I knew, of bed but only of old movies with night-club scenes.

Catholic girls were, of course, warned by the nuns that wearing makeup was not what God wanted them to do. Any girl who indicated a desire to do so was labeled by the nuns as "boy crazy." During the last five minutes of the day's final class, a "boy crazy" girl could predictably be found crunched up behind the girl sitting in front of her, hurrying to get some lipstick and rouge on before the bell rang. "Boy crazy" girls usually had "girl crazy" boys waiting to pick them up from school.

The nuns repeatedly cautioned the girls about the

danger of committing the serious sin of "Scandal," which was the sin whereby one's own actions caused someone else to sin, the "someone else" being boys, naturally. According to the nuns, it took very little on the part of a Catholic girl to have a boy go wild with lust: a skirt that was slightly too short, a perfume that was a bit too strong, a smile that was a little too friendly. Boys, said the nuns, were cruddy-minded creeps who filled all their waking hours fantasizing about females. The only time that boys didn't think about sex was when they thought about food. But the moment their stomachs were filled, they went right back to thinking about sex. That was why, claimed an old nun who taught at one of the Catholic girls' high schools, most rapes occurred near restaurants.

Sister Catherine taught freshman Religion at St. Teresa High School, which was three blocks away from Bremmer. She liked to tell her students about the dangers of early dating. "In the years ahead, you'll have plenty of time for boys," Sister Catherine used to say. "Remember, the girl who starts dating at too young of an age finds herself getting married at too young of an age."

In the opinion of Sister Catherine, the social stream that carried a young Catholic girl from casual conversation with members of the opposite sex to the altar was one that started wide and shallow and took years to run narrow and deep. She advised her students to initially limit their social contacts with boys to situations of group dating. Safety in numbers and all of that. Only after a reasonable amount of time, such as a few years, said Sister Catherine, should a girl advance to casual dating, making sure never to have more than two dates in a row with the same boy. In terms of time, this stage should be the longest step toward marriage. Only after a girl had dated a wide variety of boys should she allow herself the privilege of "serious dating." Sister Catherine defined "serious dating" as where the girl kissed the boy good night on the fourth date. Sister Catherine assured the girls that with her time schedule there was still plenty of time left for a long engagement period, marriage, a family, and celebrating one's fifty-fifth birthday.

Priests from the neighboring parishes would go to St. Teresa High School two or three times a month to teach religion classes. The ostensible reason for the nuns importing the priests was that the priests were more capable of answering the girls' difficult theological questions. Actually it was just that the priests were slightly more willing to talk "openly" about a topic that the nuns felt was rather repulsive, namely boys.

Father Bernard Rasp, who had recently been ordained, was one of those priests. As a boy Father Rasp had reached his social peak in eighth grade when he was assigned to serve midnight Mass on Christmas Eve. It was also in eighth grade that little Bernard Rasp played third-string guard for the parish grammar school basketball team. The assistant pastor, Father Baker, was the coach of the basketball team. Father Baker knew of Bernard's plans to enter the priesthood and took Bernard's interest in playing basketball as a definite sign that he had a priestly vocation. Every kid Father Baker had known who had gone on to the seminary had been a mediocre basketball player. Kids who played basketball well and those who didn't play it at all never showed any interest in becoming a priest. Father Baker was convinced that little Bernard Rasp would make it to the priesthood. Unfortunately Father Baker was right.

Bernard Rasp went straight from grammar school to the seminary and twelve years later became a priest. In his entire life he had never once dated a girl. Father Rasp considered it an act of infidelity if he ate Sunday dinner anywhere else but at mom's place.

During a sophomore religion class at St. Teresa High School, Father Rasp handed out mimeographed sheets that laid down the rules for "making out." These sheets, said Father Rasp, would help clarify what was sinful and what was not. They contained the standard information that was espoused by most of the Catholic "experts" on the topic. An "expert" was any priest, nun, or religious brother who decided to be one. Following are some of the highlights of those sheets.

Concerning Making Out, What You Should Know

It is *always* a mortal sin for unmarried people to:
1. Go all the way, together or alone;
2. Pet (feeling around in the wrong places);
3. Neck (both heads on each other's shoulders and embracing);
4. French kiss (touch tongues);
5. Kiss passionately.

When, you ask yourself, does a kiss become passionate? A kiss becomes passionate when:
1. It lasts over thirty seconds (Check your watch right now. It's a long time.);
2. There are a number of kisses with short time intervals in between. For instance, ten or more

kisses, with intervals of less than two minutes, is always too dangerous;

3. It is done in the dark, alone, or with a group of fast guys and make-outs.

It is a mortal sin to tell God by your actions that you're willing to risk hurting yourself and/or someone else seriously. That is why the five actions listed above offend Him seriously. He loves the people involved and knows that these actions hurt them.

A definite line is impossible to draw for everyone at the same time. You are the final judge of what is sinful and what is not.

Perhaps the best rule of thumb to go by in the matter of kissing is this (all you have to remember is the word FEAR):

F *f*requent kisses should not be repeated in a short time;

E *e*nduring; a kiss, outside of marriage, should not be a long one;

A *a*rdent; a kiss should not go beyond the warmth of simple friendliness;

R *r*eligion; remember your Catholic faith when you feel that you are getting into serious trouble through kissing.

Is there any way for the unmarried to kiss affectionately without committing a mortal sin? Most certainly. It is not sinful to share five or fewer kisses of five seconds or less each, with respect and realistic affection and spread over two or three hours.

Keep in mind that the only proper place for "making out" is in marriage. Remember, also, when you are on a date, that the sin of Scandal (leading another into sin) is a very serious one. Although the boy is responsible for his actions, you are the one who is really in charge.

With this kind of warm-up behind them, Catholic girls were expected to walk into the game of marriage and promptly produce twenty new Catholics apiece.

According to Father Rasp's sheets, when a Catholic girl kissed you good night it was not so important that she had a great set of lips but rather that she could handle a stopwatch. Or lacking that, she could count out loud.

For freshman Nancy Ralansky, Father Rasp's mimeographed sheets were a welcome revelation of Catholic doctrine. When Nancy was in sixth grade, the nun tol the class that if someone wanted to get to Heaven, he or she would have to do a lot of suffering here on earth, just as Christ did. Nancy Ralansky went home and, since she didn't own a cross, spent the lunch hour kneeling on her jacks. For the next two weeks Nancy spent her lunch hours kneeling on jacks. She stopped doing it only because she was beginning to enjoy the pain. Since she was now getting pleasure from kneeling on her jacks, giving it up gave her more pain, which moved her another notch closer to Heaven. Before she met Father Rasp, Nancy Ralansky believed that if you French kissed with a boy you could get pregnant. After a private conference with Father Rasp, Nancy no longer worried about giving birth to a seven-pound tongue.

Although there were many girls who were vaguely suspicious that Father Rasp might be a little off center, there were only a few who were convinced that his sexual sophistication was barely at the subsistence level. They were the ones who set him up with stupid questions, such as "Is it a sin to wear sleeveless dresses?" But Father Rasp was well prepared for them. He gave stupid answers. "Yes, it is."

Father Rasp spent many religion classes talking about the dangers of going steady. He never used that precise term because he had never heard it. Father Rasp referred to it instead as "consistently keeping company with the same boy." Like most authorities on teen-agers, Father Rasp did not believe that "familiarity breeds contempt" but rather simply that "familiarity breeds."

During all my young dating years, the thirst of my sex drive went unquenched. One night, after a particularly frustrating date, I dreamed that all the girls in my Catholic world had been stored behind a number of barriers. The first one was a huge wall of brick and mortar. A fortress of such muscle that it made the China Wall look like a shoestring. Behind that were the members of the Chicago Police Department, all of whom had just had their latest request for a pay raise turned down by the mayor. They were backed up by a crowd made up entirely of army recruiters and possessive mothers. And standing behind all of that was God Himself.

Today, finally, all the barriers are down. There are willing targets everywhere. Not that it matters. The old bomb, it ain't what it used to be.

Poof.

THE BEAUTIFUL WORLD OF
RICHARD BOBBO

At Bremmer High School everyone liked everyone else. Almost. No one liked the fat and ugly kids. Like every society, Bremmer High School had its scapegoats.

There really wasn't anyone else to pick on. When it came to minority students, Bremmer was in a bad way. Being a Catholic high school, it didn't have any Jews. In addition, Bremmer was all-White even though it had twelve Black students.

At that time the only Blacks who bothered going to Bremmer were the "White Blacks." I mean, they looked Black, but they talked White and they thought White. For all practical purposes, they were White. One of them, Teddy Collins, was so White he even played the accordion.

The only real Black person in the school was Raymond the janitor. I don't know what Raymond's last name was. No one did, including Raymond.

If cleanliness is truly next to Godliness, then Bremmer High School was a suburb of Heaven. Raymond was a compulsive cleaner. He even sprayed Lysol on his breakfast cereal. Although Raymond never looked that neat himself, his school (Raymond always referred to Bremmer as "his school") was impeccable. Some students claimed that Raymond had acquired his hygienic habits at one of the various prisons where he supposedly had done time. Regardless of where Raymond learned, he learned well.

Raymond was the only janitor the school had. A few students picked up extra money by helping Raymond after school and on Saturday, and the cooks in the cafeteria took care of the kitchen. But outside of those minor servings of help, it was Raymond alone who kept Bremmer High School squeaky clean.

Raymond achieved this feat by getting the complete cooperation of all 1,600 students. A cooperation that was based on each student's assumption that Raymond was quite willing to destroy anyone who would dare to defile his school with dirt.

On rainy or sloppy days he would lay down a number of rubber mats on the floor, just inside the main door. Raymond would then stand there and give the word to each student as he arrived. "Hey, wipe those feet good. This ain't no shithouse, man. Hey, you, get back here. You still got shit all over those shoes." Raymond's style was so Black that everyone, including the twelve Black students, referred to him as "that nigger."

Even if there had been some Jews and Blacks around Bremmer High School, they wouldn't have been bothered. Using members of minority groups as coat hangers was already becoming an "out" thing to do. Too obvious. So everybody picked on the fat and ugly kids instead.

The highest form of life at Bremmer High School was the athlete, who demanded and got nothing less than complete adoration from both faculty and students alike. Everyone on the football team, even the fourth stringers, was considered an "athlete." But in any other sport, with the possible exception of basketball, you had to be a star at it before you were generally recognized as an "athlete."

Second in social prestige to the athletes were the nuts who had school spirit, "suck spirit" as Felix Lindor used to call it. These were the students who joined eighty billion extracurricular activities, attended all school functions, including the library club meetings on Thursday nights, and genuflected every morning on the front steps before coming into school.

The athletes and the school-spirit nuts were the ones whose faces made multiple appearances in the yearbook. The same situation existed with the school newspaper, *The Bremmer Weekly*. The school-spirit nuts who worked on it—"wrote" would hardly be the word to use—devoted most of the newspaper space to their three favorite topics: the athletes, the faculty, and themselves.

No matter what a faculty member did, a school-spirit nut could justify it. If a teacher gave a test based entirely on footnotes, a school-spirit nut would say that, after all, why would an author bother putting in footnotes that could only be read with a microscope if they weren't important?

If you were neither an athlete nor a school-spirit nut, but you still wanted to be socially accepted by them and the faculty, or at least not be bothered by any of the three, then you became a "nice guy." The vast majority of students at Bremmer were "nice guys." They spent their four years smiling at everything that moved and at a few things that didn't. This constant exposure of enamel usually insured the bearer against being deliberately messed up by the athletes, the faculty, or the school-spirit nuts.

The lowest rung on Bremmer's social ladder, the one that everybody automatically stepped on in order to feel a little taller, was made up of the fat and ugly kids. If you were just fat, and you were jovial all the time, you could usually pass yourself off as a clown of sorts. If you were just ugly, but tough besides, you wouldn't be bothered either. No one likes getting his nose flattened. But if you were fat *and* ugly, you didn't have a prayer. Fat *and* ugly kids are never funny or tough. They are just fat and ugly.

Even the faculty picked on the fat and ugly kids. In the "flunkable" subjects such as the foreign languages, math courses, and physical sciences, an unofficial quota system was observed. About ten percent of the class was destined to go under. But teachers never flunked athletes or school-spirit nuts. Even "nice guys" were rarely subjected to summer school. The slack had to be taken up by somebody. That doomed ten percent was almost always stuffed solidly with fat and ugly kids. Very few teachers at Bremmer High School did not subscribe to a "flunk the freaks" philosophy.

Bremmer, like most high schools, had a detention system. If you displeased a faculty member in any way, he could assign you to "detention," which among the students was more commonly referred to as "jug." Jug consisted of sitting in Room 107 for an hour after school and doing absolutely nothing. No studying, no sleeping, no anything.

In giving you detention the faculty member would fill out a detention slip, which provided spaces for the date, the name of the student offender, and the name of the faculty member. Below all this were four columns of various offenses that could land a person in jug, such as "failure to do homework," "no tie," and "tardiness." The faculty member simply had to check the appropriate one.

Actually, no one ever went to jug for not wearing a tie because many students kept extra ties in their lockers and rented them out to the guys who kept forgetting to wear one. You could tell, however, if a tie was rented. It looked like it had gone through someone's digestive tract.

A visit to the jug room any day after school would have revealed a heavy population of fat and ugly kids with a sprinkling of "nice guys" who hadn't been quite nice enough that day. Under ideal conditions, a fat and ugly kid, open full throttle, could pick up seven or eight detentions in a single day. There were many athletes and school-spirit nuts, though, who went through all four years without ever once being jugged. I knew one fat and ugly kid who insisted that if anyone had the time to read through all the offenses listed on a detention slip, he would find one that simply said "fat and ugly."

Fat and ugly kids never joined the yearbook staff or had their names appear in the school newspaper "gossip" columns. They were never seen at football games, basketball games, sock hops, or any gathering of over three. Fat and ugly kids participated in virtually none of the school's extracurricular activities and were often accused of having no school spirit even though the bookstore didn't carry any sizes of "Bremmer High School" jackets that would fit a fat and ugly kid.

There might have been some fat and ugly kids on the debating team but, at the time I went to Bremmer, there was no way of knowing. Being on the debating team was considered such a social stigma that all its members remained incognito. Three years after I graduated, one of its members, Basil Flaherty, came out of the closet and, as a parting shot, exposed the names of his fellow debaters. Three of them sued Basil for defamation of character, and won.

With close friends such as Lanner, Heidi, and Felix Lindor, I could never figure out what sections of the Bremmer social system they were stuck in. It's tough to label people you know well. You can see too many different things in them.

I had no such doubts about myself. I was definitely a fat and ugly kid, at least internally. On the outside I wasn't fat at all. In fact, I was skinny. And I was only mildly ugly. But internally I thought like a fat and ugly kid and therefore, most of the time, was treated like one. There were a few other kids in the school like me. Not many, though. The typical fat and ugly kid was fat and ugly on both sides of his skin.

During the two minutes between class periods, the halls of Bremmer High School would almost burst with students hustling to their next class. They would rumble through the halls, cheerfully spraying out typical high school greetings as they passed one another, banging heads into lockers, shoulder-punching, goosing. Overall, it was a delightful two minutes of being alive.

Except for the fat and ugly kids. They would instead chug along close to the walls, lips silent, heads bowed. Fat fingers would wrap around their books in the hope of deterring someone in search of a cheap thrill from knocking the books out of their hands.

Elections were always a mock at Bremmer High School. Each homeroom had its own class representative and he was inevitably a fat and ugly kid. The worst thing that could happen to someone at Bremmer was to be elected president of the student council. That meant he wasn't just a fat and ugly kid but *the* fattest and ugliest kid in the entire school.

The real student power at Bremmer High School was in the hideous hands of—who else but the athletes? They were the ones who decided what things should or should not be done. The fat and ugly kids just went along and did what the athletes told them to do, except for one fat and ugly kid who was so fat and so ugly that he was twice elected a class representative and was once nominated for the presidency of the student council. Richard Bobbo.

At the moment of birth fate had played a lousy trick on Richard Bobbo. It allowed him to survive. Richard had so much dandruff that it was beginning to take over his forehead, and a case of acne that got worse as you watched it. His stomach was so huge that it had literally been years since he had last seen his feet. By the time Richard Bobbo got to high school, his toes were little more than a rumor to him.

His parents constantly worried about what everyone else thought of their son, though Richard Bobbo had a suspicion that it was better they didn't know. The only people who would hang around with Richard Bobbo were other fat and ugly kids and he didn't care what they thought of him. He realized they were lepers together.

According to the philosophy of the athletic department at Bremmer High School, if you could put a ball through a hoop, you were physically fit. Therefore twenty out of the fifty-eight minutes of every gym class were spent playing basketball. Each guy spent the other thirty-eight minutes undressing and jamming his clothes into a locker the size of a midget's fedora, putting on a gym suit he hadn't washed in three years, running out onto the gym floor and answering roll call, listening to the latest crude joke from the coach, making sure to guffaw loud and long when the punch line came so that no one would think he was simpleminded or queer, running back to the locker room after the twenty minutes of basketball, taking a shower in a communal stall reminiscent of Auschwitz movies, nervously waiting for one of his demented classmates to either try and scald his skin off with a blast of hot water or to knock every nerve out of his body with a spray of cold water, attempting to dry himself off with a postage-stamp towel provided courtesy of Bremmer High School, and then putting his street clothes back on, which having been compressed in that four-inch cubicle of a locker, had mildewed around his wallet in the back pocket.

Fat and ugly kids never took gym; nor, like other students, did they have to give excuses to the coach for not doing so. If a normal person wanted to skip gym, he would have to bring a note from his family doctor stating that he was suffering from a terminal disease and that playing basketball was detrimental to his health. But fat and ugly kids didn't have to bother with notes. They just didn't take gym. The reason, though never officially stated, was apparent. Why get everyone else sick to their stomachs by having naked fat and ugly kids all over the locker room?

During gym classes the fat and ugly kids were assigned menial tasks by the coach to keep them out of trouble. Richard Bobbo was always given the job of handing out the four-inch-square towels to the guys after they had come in from the gym floor and had taken their showers.

The towels were kept in a wire cage to prevent anyone from using more than his allotted one. The wire cage had a window through which the towels could be handed and a door that could be locked only from the inside.

One day a group of sweaty slobs came running in from the gym floor to the locker room, undressed, showered, and began lining up in front of the wire cage for their towels. Richard Bobbo was standing inside the cage, pivoting and twisting his tubby torso as he grabbed towels from the stack behind him and jammed them into grasping hands, which stretched through the wire cage window.

For the first seven guys, all went well. Hand out, towel in hand, hand out, towel in hand, hand out, towel in hand. The eighth guy in line was known by everyone in Bremmer High School. His name was Bert Bensen. That wasn't his full name. His full name was Bert the Beast Bensen. He was seven feet tall and seven feet wide. A walking cube of Kryptonite. Bert the Beast Bensen resembled a freight car not only in shape but in strength and intelligence as well. The school newspaper often referred to Bert as a "gifted athlete."

Naked, Bert the Beast stood in front of the wire cage and stuck his hand through the window. "Hey, Bobbo, hurry up with that towel," he shouted.

Richard Bobbo, seeing who was now standing at the cage window, folded both arms on his bulging belly and just stared at Bensen. The beast bellowed again.

"Bobbo, you bastard, hurry up with that goddamn towel."

Richard Bobbo, five feet, three inches, 183 'pounds, two of them pure dandruff, whose award-winning acne had earned him numerous contract offers from cosmetic companies, replied very loudly and very slowly in a voice so shrill it was approximately two decibels away from being out of human-hearing range.

"Fuck you."

The beast was stunned. It was probably the first time in his life that he had an insult hit him head on. Certainly the first time for him stark naked. The locker room was suddenly silent. A few were tempted to laugh but decided against it in the interest of good health.

Bert the Beast grabbed at the wire cage. "Bobbo, you lousy sonofabitch, I'm gonna crush that lousy pimply head of yours against the wall."

Richard Bobbo lifted one of his hands, which had been resting complacently on his belly. The hand curled into a fist. One finger slowly stood, silently repeating Richard Bobbo's message to Bert the Beast Bensen.

Bert the Beast became so enraged that he started to climb through the wire cage window. He somehow managed to get his massive naked frame about a third of the way through when he realized that if he made one more move, forward or backward, he would castrate himself. He would be Bert Bensen, minus the beast.

Richard Bobbo decided that it was as good a time as any to leave. He swung open the wire cage door and waddled across the locker room floor in a style somewhere between a John Wayne stride and a James Cagney strut, pushing stunned naked bodies out of his path. A few cronies were attempting to ease Bert the Beast out of the wire cage window with as little damage as possible. So ended Round One.

For the next five months, Richard Bobbo was a hunted man. Bert the Beast didn't dare go after Richard during school hours. It would have been too humiliating for Bert to admit that he was actually willing to touch anything as disgusting as Richard Bobbo. So for five months, outside of school, Bert the Beast Bensen hunted Richard Bobbo.

Richard wasn't an easy man to get, for as Bert the Beast discovered, Richard Bobbo could run. You see, Richard Bobbo seemed to be the end product of an orgy rather than of parenthood. His body was made up of at least twenty nonfitting parts. Two of those parts were the extremely overdeveloped calves in his legs. They looked like Goodyear blimps hanging below his knees. His overdeveloped calves enabled Richard, despite his five-foot, three-inch, 183-pound mass, to be able to run like a banshee for about fifty feet before his internal system totally collapsed. Richard Bobbo made it a point never to be farther away than fifty feet from a sanctuary, be it home, school, or church. A showdown had to come, and it did—in, of all places, the school cafeteria.

The only difference between the Bremmer High School cafeteria and the zoo was that the cafeteria had more animals. Upon entering it, all pretense of being human was dropped. Every year a few guys would shove it in so fast they'd lose a couple of fingers. In the Bremmer cafeteria you could call a guy's mother anything you wanted, but you'd better not threaten to touch his food.

After eating, or what passed for it, students were expected to stack their plates and silverware on tables in the kitchen of the cafeteria. Then they were to carry all their garbage on their trays, such as brown bags, bread crusts, and banana peels, over to a huge open-mouth chute in a corner of the cafeteria. There they were to slide their garbage off their trays into the chute.

But the Bremmer High School students, being of a practical nature, decided it would be much easier to just go to the chute and throw everything in, silverware and dishes included. What they'd do is hide the stuff in their brown bags and fling it down there.

In an attempt to put a stop to the mass murder of dinnerware, the school administration assigned Raymond the janitor to sit in the basement, directly below the chute, and feel up all the brown bags that came down. If he found plates or silverware he was to buzz an electronic bell, which was located directly above the chute upstairs in the cafeteria. When that bell rang, two members of the kitchen crew would come sweeping out of the cafeteria kitchen and carry off the culprit to Brother Purity's office and a three-day suspension.

Among the hundreds of students at Bremmer High School, someone would have eventually thought of it, but fortunately for Richard Bobbo, he was the first.

Over at Table Seven, Row A, on the end chair, sat Bert the Beast Bensen, who had just finished his third lunch in the past twenty minutes. Bert had deliberately eaten less than usual because his mother was making his favorite dish for supper that night—old warehouses. He was scrupulously separating his silverware and plate and placing them on one side of his tray and then pushing all his paper waste to the other side of the tray. Bert, though a beast, was a neat beast. There were only three minutes left until the end of the lunch period and students were skittering all over the place, trying to get to their homerooms before the next period began.

Bert the Beast Bensen realized that someone was standing over his shoulder. He looked up slowly at a porkly pimply pile of flesh better known as Richard Bobbo. Richard was carrying a tray that was loaded with lunch bags crammed with garbage. Fat and ugly kids were often used as convenient crud couriers by their classmates. Richard Bobbo attempted to smile but his lips couldn't coordinate their efforts.

"Say, Bert," Richard Bobbo squeaked, "I'm on my way over to the chute and I've got a lot of other guys' bags here. Let me take yours for you."

"You lousy sonofabitch, I oughta throw you down that chute." Obviously, the revenge of Bert the Beast Bensen was not going to be satisfied merely by the removal of a couple of bags of garbage. But while Bert the Beast was talking, Richard Bobbo had picked up the two bags of garbage and had placed them on his own tray.

"Put my lunch bags back on my tray, Bobbo," Bert the Beast graveled menacingly.

"Okay, Bert, okay." Richard Bobbo picked the two lunch bags out of the heap on his tray and dropped them back on Bert the Beast's tray. Then, once again, Richard Bobbo began slowly plodding toward the garbage chute, his feet alternately shuffling and halting in an attempt to keep all the brown bags on his tray.

Bert the Beast Bensen, after rearranging his plate, knife, and fork for the final time, walked to the tables in the kitchen and deposited his dinnerware. He next went over to the garbage chute and butted his way into the front of the line of guys waiting to get rid of their garbage. Bert the Beast then slid his two lunch bags off the tray and into the chute.

He was just putting his tray on the pile next to the chute when the bell above it went off. Within the second jigger of the ring, the line of guys had disappeared. The cafeteria was empty. Bert the Beast Bensen stood alone. Two men from the kitchen crew, bigger and meaner-looking than even Bert the Beast, stomped out from the cafeteria kitchen and each clamped on to one of Bert the Beast's arms.

"There must be somethin' wrong with that bell. I didn't throw no plates or silverware away." But up from the basement came the voice of Raymond the janitor: "Two knives and a fork hidden in the bags."

If you go back to Bremmer High School today and ask among the students if they've heard of Bert the Beast Bensen, you'll probably find no one who has. Every class has its hero athletes and all hero athletes are pretty much the same.

But if you go back and slither among the fat and ugly kids with the name of Richard Bobbo on your lips, they will remember. For he was one of theirs who dared defy—a flame of hope in that four-year cesspool along the sewer of life. And they will remember that for his courage Richard Bobbo was paid the highest honor possible to a fat and ugly kid by his fellow students. After his cafeteria coup, Richard Bobbo was never again even nominated to a student office.

5

MY SISTER WAS A PIANO FREAK

Somewhere in the November of my sophomore year, standing in the basement on a late Saturday afternoon. Heart beating fast, my body smothered with sweat, I was near exhaustion. The arm muscles continued to flicker from the assault they had just executed. My hand still held the sharp-edged weapon. Looking down at it, puzzled by how I could have enjoyed doing such a thing. Trying to justify it in my mind. Telling myself that it wasn't my fault if my older sister was a piano freak.

When I was a kid, taking music lessons was one of the best ways of showing all the adults around you that you weren't really interested in being a kid and that, instead, you wanted to be an adult as fast as you could. Adults love that kind of stuff. They call it "maturity." Most kids call if something else. My older sister had "maturity." She was forty-five years old on the day she was born.

Like most piano freaks, my sister started young. With only a few days of first grade behind her, she entered St. Bastion Grammar School's music program, which consisted of one upright church organ, one upright piano, and one upright nun.

Sister Helen, the music teacher, was a very nice person, but her knowledge of music was somewhat limited. My sister came home ecstatic from her first piano lesson and immediately repeated the words of Sister Helen to the rest of the family. "These are the white keys. These are the black keys. See you next week, kid."

One good thing about Sister Helen, though. She almost wiped out my sister. Sister Helen demanded that her students play the piano with their hands arched, just their finger tips touching the keys, their arms close to their bodies and their legs stretched so that their toes could constantly hover over the foot pedals. Since my sister was only about four feet tall at that age, she had a tough time doing all that contorting and stretching. Sister Helen had her looking like a Slinky on the verge of a seizure.

After a few years of taking lessons from Sister Helen, my sister went on to other musical mentors. There was Mrs. Babkowski, who had a head as big as a barrel, which sat atop a fireplug neck. Her head and neck rested on shoulders that looked as if they had been chopped out of granite. But the weird thing about Mrs. Babkowski was that almost all of her weight seemed to be in her shoulders and above. From her armpits on down, she couldn't have weighed more than twelve pounds. When Mrs. Babkowski wore a red hat, she looked like an expired parking meter.

Even though Mrs. Babkowski was quite a sight herself, she had a frenzied fear of virtually everything in existence. She used my sister's piano lessons to talk about such fears.

Mrs. Babkowski once spent eight dollars' worth of piano lessons lecturing on how she wouldn't teach anyone to play musical instruments that vibrated against them because she knew that such instruments caused heart attacks. Mrs. Babkowski based this knowledge on the fact that a neighbor of hers had dropped dead while picking at a ukulele.

Mrs. Babkowski also felt that the world would soon end because of an overabundance of shopping centers. She reasoned that the earth would become so cluttered with them that there would be no room left to grow any food and most of us would starve to death as we wandered aimlessly around in some Sears, Roebuck.

My sister also took piano lessons from Mr. Kelly. With him, my sister not only received music lessons for her $2.50 an hour, but she also got to play in his band, which was composed of all the students Mr. Kelly taught. The band included nine accordions, four piano players and one piano, two tubas, some drums, a banjo, and a Hawaiian guitar.

Geraldine Hasher was Mr. Kelly's favorite student. She played "lead" accordion and practiced "Lady of Spain" twenty hours a day. Geraldine's hands were always on her accordion, even when she wasn't playing it. Although she was only a fifth grader, Geraldine stood five feet, nine inches tall. But she only weighed fifty pounds. With that accordion strapped around her shoulders all the time, Geraldine Hasher was slowly bending to the law of gravity, in the process becoming the Quasimodo of Mr. Kelly's band.

One of the piano players was Eddie Feinstein. Eddie's family spent nearly four thousand dollars and seven years on Eddie's piano endeavors. Today Eddie is an insurance man with a forehead that is currently racing back to meet his neck. All Eddie has to show for that four thousand dollars and seven years is one weary rendition of "White Christmas," a song that is played during only one season of the year. Eddie doesn't even bother to play it then, since he's Jewish.

Ernest O'Shea played the banjo in Mr. Kelly's band. The banjo had been left to him by his uncle. According to Ernest, his uncle also left him Ernest's aunt. But Ernest chose to bring the banjo to band practice. He didn't think his aunt would blend well with a Hawaiian guitar.

Each spring Mr. Kelly would give a concert for all the parents in order to convince them that they weren't really wasting their money.

At the signal, two taps on the podium by Mr. Kelly's baton, the band's fourteen instruments would simultaneously begin moaning as they stumbled toward what Mr. Kelly hoped would be a melody.

About ten seconds into the number, each band member would begin playing his own version of the song. Some would play a little faster than the others. Some would play louder. And some, like Joe Hans on the drums, would get bored with the whole scene and stop playing altogether. Throughout the song, Mr. Kelly would wave his baton wildly above his head as if he were making cotton candy.

To signal the end, Mr. Kelly would suddenly stick out his arms in such a way that he would give more than a few parents the impression that he was going to try to fly. Mr. Kelly would then swing his arms in a wide arch, forcing his hands to smack together in a loud clap. Hearing the midair collision, most of the band members would immediately stop playing. There were usually a few, however, who were thirty or forty seconds late. Geraldine Hasher, who definitely had something going with her accordion, was always the last to stop playing.

Only one of Mr. Kelly's annual concerts resulted in a near fatality. Jimmy Flickmore was in the middle of his tuba solo, "Ave Maria," when a strong westerly wind abruptly changed directions and flushed down Jimmy's tuba. The last three notes of the song were played on Jimmy by the tuba. Seconds later, Jimmy Flickmore managed to pull his lips away from the mouthpiece. Otherwise the tuba might well have blown him to bits.

A few years after my sister started taking lessons, my father decided to buy her a piano. He didn't, of course, just race out to the nearest piano store and buy one. Such major purchases demanded major efforts. The entire family spent six months of weekends tromping through old warehouses stuffed with aging, dusty, disabled pianos, looking for one worthy of my sister's talents. Eventually we found it; a sticky-pedal, skinny-leg, beaten-brown upright. Its varnish was scraggly with age, its cover couldn't quite get over its keys, and the middle "C" didn't work. It was the perfect piano for my sister. It looked like she sounded.

Noticing all the attention my sister was getting from the rest of the family because of her musical endeavors, I decided to give her some competition. I had heard somewhere that there are people who are so musically talented they can play a musical instrument "by ear." They don't even have to practice on it. I had a feeling that I was such a gifted person.

I went to the dime store and bought a harmonica. Sure enough, I discovered on the way home that I could easily play it by ear. Boy, was my sister stupid. Here she had spent years and a lot of my father's money learning how to play a musical instrument, and I had just accomplished the same thing in less time than it took me to walk home from Woolworth's. I was even thinking of writing some original music for my harmonica. "Blow, pause, pause, pause, blow, blow, pause, blow. . . ."

When I walked into the house, I could hear my sister plunking away in the basement. I went downstairs, walked over to the piano, and waved at her to stop playing.

"What do you want now?" she yelled over the crashing of the keys.

I held the harmonica up in the air. "Listen for a second," I shouted. "I can play this by ear."

Her fingers froze on the keys while her eyes leaped to the ceilings of their sockets as she faked a frenzied state of exasperation. "Hurry up," she blurted, "I haven't got all day."

My cheeks, with the reluctant cooperation of my lips, promptly puffed out a snappy version of "I'm Looking over a Four Leaf Clover."

"What do you think of that?" I gasped as I tried to regain my breath.

"I suggest," said my sister stiffly, "that rather than playing your harmonica by ear, you stick it in your ear."

I have since discovered that most piano players are like my sister, real egomaniacs. They're always telling you about how the piano is the "most perfect" of musical instruments and how you have to be blessed with "piano hands" in order to play the piano well. Harmonica players, however, are very humble people. You never hear a harmonica player going around bragging about having a "harmonica mouth."

My sister was sensational at messing up family gatherings. No sooner would everyone be settling down to have a good time than my mother would ruin it by announcing that my sister was going to provide some musical entertainment for us. Only those who were lucky enough to be within the sanctity of the bathroom when the announcement came stood any chance of survival. They would simply lock the door and answer all summonses with flushes and silence.

The rest of the clan would be herded down the stairs and into the basement. There, amid the soiled paper plates, half-eaten potato salad, and lukewarm beer, my mother would inform the relatives that my sister was going to play a few of her "favorites" for us.

My mother would then make it a point to mention how long my sister had been taking lessons: five years, six years, whatever it was. My mother did that in order to make it clear to my relatives that what they were about to hear was the result of many years of determined effort. So even before my sister began playing my relatives knew she was a good piano player, even if she didn't sound like one.

My sister would start out her concert with a few practice scales. She was good on those. She would then play "Buttons and Bows." Unfortunately, the section of the keyboard used in "Buttons and Bows" had a few keys that no longer worked. The melody was thus constantly interrupted by soft, noteless plunks. If you closed your eyes while my sister played that song, and my relatives had a habit of closing their eyes regardless of the song, it sounded like the piano was hiccuping.

My sister always wrapped up with "God Bless America." It was a finale that benefited everyone. It guaranteed my sister a standing ovation since most of my relatives thought it was the national anthem, or at least they weren't sure enough that it wasn't.

It was a good deal for them, too. It put them on their feet for a quick getaway, which was sometimes necessary. My sister would often get a swelled head from the sprinkling of applause, which usually accompanied the standing ovation, and would try to lay another song on them.

Many beautiful changes occur within a girl as she blooms from childhood to womanhood. If she's a piano freak, one of the most beautiful changes is that she slowly, but almost always, gives up playing the piano.

My sister was no exception. By the time she was a senior in high school she hardly ever practiced at all, which was just as well. By then most of the piano's keys, at least those that still worked, sounded the same. On those now rare occasions that my sister did play the piano, even she didn't know what song she was playing. The piano had gone completely tone-deaf.

On a Saturday afternoon my sister's musical career ran out of notes. That morning my father told me to take the piano out of the basement and put it in the alley for the garbage men to pick up. A few weeks earlier, when the basement had flooded, the piano had managed to get two of its pedals permanently waterlogged. Now, besides hiccuping whenever it was played and having all of its workable keys sound the same, it also gurgled. That was too much even for my sister. She didn't cry or carry on nearly as loud as I thought she would when she heard my father telling me to get rid of it.

My first question was "How?" It had taken my father, three uncles, two neighbors, four quarts of beer, a sprained back, and a near-hernia to get the piano into the basement. My father handed me a very simple solution—an axe.

I spent the whole Saturday afternoon chopping up my sister's piano. In a way I liked doing it. I was at that age where I could enjoy chopping up a piano. Actually, I would have enjoyed chopping up anything.

But in another way, I felt lousy about it. I kept seeing the piano as the brand-new one it had been a long time ago. There wasn't a thing wrong with it, then. It was absolutely perfect. It even smelled new. I imagined some little girl of years ago giggling with delight at the sight of her new piano. That little girl was an old lady now, probably rotting away in some nursing home. And here I was, chopping up her piano.

I envisioned the piano going from one owner to the next until it finally landed in that old warehouse. There it sat for months, wondering whether it would ever again feel the flow of fingers on its keys. Then my sister and our family came along and gave that old piano a brand-new shot of life. A life that I was now ending with my axe.

It was getting damp and dark by the time I dragged the last piece, a large heavy section of metal that had lain deep in the heart of the piano, out to the alley. After dropping the metal onto the heap of the dismembered piano, I ran back to the house and into the kitchen for a drink of water. My father was there, looking for something in the "junk" drawer.

"I feel kind of bad about chopping up the piano," I said to him. "You know, that thing might have been good for another couple of years." I placed the empty glass in the sink and began walking across the kitchen toward the basement stairs. The residue of my savagery still remained to be cleaned up.

"Look at it this way," said my father. "It went out on a high note."

"What do you mean?" I stopped and asked.

"It sounded better today than it has in years."

6

MIXERS

Since most Catholic high schools were not coeducational, the only systematic way of meeting members of the opposite sex was at those weekend rituals that went under a variety of names, such as "socials," "sock hops," and that most frequently used tag, "mixers." Regardless of what they were called they all referred to basically the same thing: a few frantic hours of searching for some friendly flesh.

A mixer was where you went and worried all night that everyone was going to notice the pimple on your chin. In fact nobody ever did because they were all too busy worrying about the pimples on their own chins.

Mixers were usually held on Friday nights in the school basements of various parishes, high school gymnasiums, and, occasionally, in meeting halls of civic groups such as the "Moose." Bremmer High School never held mixers because it didn't want to compete with the local parishes, most of which did have them.

I'd normally go to a mixer with two or three of my friends hoping to meet the girl of my dreams, and I'd spend all night talking to my two or three friends.

Most mixers were a bonanza for the electric company. The chaperones kept the room so bright that you thought they had brought in the sun. If you went to enough mixers, you could keep your tan right through the winter.

Mixers were highly segregated. On the fast numbers the dance floor was thinly populated. A few guys would be out there, but quite a number of the couples would be girls dancing with one another. Most of the guys stood along one wall while the majority of girls did the same thing along the opposite wall. The girls silently wondered why all the boys acted like babies while, on the other side of the room, each boy hoped that the next number would be a "slow song." Most of the boys thought they looked like idiots when they danced "fast." They were right.

Whenever two people danced with each other for the first time, the same questions automatically sprang from their mouths. "What's your name?" "Where do you go to school?" "What year are you in?" "Say, do you know . . . ? No? Well, do you know . . . ?"

One thing you never did at a mixer was admit to anyone that you wanted to be there. If you started dancing with someone, one of your first comments would be, "I don't usually come to these things but George, my friend over there, didn't want to come alone and he kind of talked me into it." George would spend the first moments with a new dancing partner telling her the same story about you.

The quality of mixers was subject to seasonal change. The best mixers were in the autumn when most of the population was unattached and anxious to start out the new school year with a new love interest. By spring, however, when many had already found their true love—at least true enough to last them through the summer—and many others had tired of going to mixers and watching the ice in their cokes melt, the ones who did show up were a sad group indeed. Those who attended the last few mixers of the school year knew exactly how the animals felt that had been left behind by Noah.

For me, there were moments when mixers could be very depressing affairs. At least once during the night I'd ask some girl to dance and she'd say, "No, thank you" with such a strained effort that she sounded like she was trying not to get sick to her stomach. I'd hardly be turning around when she'd already be accepting a similar invitation from some guy who looked like he'd been made out of shredded wheat. Then it would be my turn to get sick to my stomach as I realized the caliber of competition that had just beaten me out. At the same time I'd be reminding myself to talk to one of the parish priests after Sunday morning Mass about the possibility of my having a vocation.

I didn't go to mixers until my sophomore year, mainly because none of my friends started going till then. Besides, there wasn't much point in attending a mixer when I was a freshman since I would have been younger than, or at best the same age as, most of the girls there. When you're a freshman, the major part of your meat market is still in grammar school.

It was an unwritten law of God that you did not mess around with an older girl. Even if you wanted to there wasn't a chance. No older girl in her right mind would risk scarring her social complexion by associating with a younger guy. Many girls, especially the ones who were stuck-up, didn't even like being seen with guys who were the same age as they were. Timmy Heidi told me that every older girl he met at a mixer reminded him of his older sister, and he didn't even have one.

Once I made the mistake of dancing with a girl who was two years older than me. When I found out how old she was, that was just the way I felt, as if I had danced with my older sister. I mean, seriously danced with her.

It didn't matter how old you were physically, but rather how old you were in school years. You could be a sophomore who was chronologically as old as most juniors, but you were still treated as a sophomore. There were no exceptions to this rule. If you were ninety-three years old, but a freshman, you could still forget about dating sophomore girls.

In September of my sophomore year Tom Lanner and I went to our first mixer. It was held in the basement of our own parish school, St. Bastion. It was a typical mixer. The admission charge was fifty cents. Soft drinks could be bought at the refreshment stand, which consisted of a card table in a corner, and music was provided by a wilted record player hypoed by a pooped-out public address system.

An hour after Lanner and I arrived, I asked a girl named Linda Luenza to dance with me. Unknowingly I violated Rule Number One of the Mixer Manual: "Never ask a girl to dance whom you've viewed only from the back."

From that angle Linda Luenza looked fantastic. Long thick brown hair plummeted in waves down her back. She had a small waist and nicely shaped legs. When I simultaneously stepped in front of her and asked her to dance, I saw that she wore her hair in uneven bangs that grew right into her eyes. She had no breasts, a slight pot belly, and chubby knees. When she smiled and said, "Yes," I noticed that her teeth looked like fingernails. Too bad for Linda and the rest of the world that she couldn't go through life with her back to it.

Naturally it was a slow song. As we began dancing, I discovered that Linda Luenza was the first girl I had ever met who was a worse dancer than I was. She moved as if she had no knees. I started going through the first dance ritual.

"What's your name?"

"Linda."

"Linda what?"

"Linda Luenza. Do you own any turtles?"

"My name's Eddie . . . what did you say?"

"I said, do you own any turtles?"

"Turtles?"

"Yes, turtles."

"No, why?"

"I own nineteen of them. Would you like to know their names?"

"Uh, all nineteen of them?"

"There's Frederick, my father bought him for me when I was only four years old. He was the very first turtle I owned. Then there's Guam, I got him when I was five. Sampson, who's only got three feet. Frederick chewed one of them off. Albany, who sleeps most of the time. . . ."

When the song ended she was on turtle number seventeen. By then Linda Luenza was beginning to look like a turtle. The instant the music stopped, I dropped both arms to my side and said, "Thank you, excuse me, but I told a friend of mine I was gonna meet him over there in the corner after this dance."

That was a lie. Lanner was standing less than twenty

feet away from me, talking to a couple of guys that we went to school with. I just wanted to get as far away as fast as possible. Whenever I get nervous I perspire like crazy. As I stood in front of Linda Luenza, I could feel my armpits melting into mush. I was sure that, by now, the ring of sweat under my arms was approaching my waist.

Linda Luenza looked shocked by my departure announcement. She being a woman, I thought she found it unbearable to part with the magnetism of my masculinity.

"You mean," she asked incredulously, "you don't want to hear about Jerky and Mable? I named him Jerky because that's the kind of meat that I feed all of them, Beef Jerky. . . ."

I turned away from Linda Luenza and quickly began walking toward the washroom, which was in the opposite corner of the school basement. The only thing I knew about turtles was that my mother would never allow one in the house. She told us that she had read somewhere that one turtle could be the carrier of as many as eighty million germs. Pushing open the washroom door as I kept my hands—the hands that had just had contact with Linda Luenza—as far away from the rest of my body as possible. Hoping that the dispenser wouldn't be out of soap and trying to multiply eighty million by nineteen.

The following Friday night Tom Lanner and I, along with Gordon Feldameano, a kid we knew from school, went again to the St. Bastion mixer. That night I met Dolores Crosley.

In the following months I would discover that Dolores Crosley had no interests or disinterests, didn't particularly like or dislike anyone, played no sports, had no hobbies, never smiled, never frowned, possessed no virtues or vices, didn't think much, didn't read much, didn't live much, and didn't breathe much. If personality were water, you could have run through Dolores Crosley and not have even gotten wet. She did, however, have one saving quality. One that made up for everything else. Dolores Crosley was gorgeous.

There is a girl like Dolores Crosley at almost every mixer. She is so attractive that she doesn't have to bother going to mixers. She could meet enough guys to keep her busy for a year just by going out on the front porch to pick up the morning newspaper. But she likes going to mixers anyway. Being with all those common, ordinary, blah people makes her feel even more beautiful. Girls like Dolores Crosley make it a point to hang around with a group of fat and ugly girls.

That night at St. Bastion's, though, Dolores Crosley was with only one fat and ugly girl. The standard procedure in such a situation was that one guy asked the gorgeous girl to dance while one of his friends asked the same of the fat and ugly girl. If you just asked the gorgeous girl, she would give you the excuse that, gee, she'd like to, but right now she was talking to her friend. So one of your friends had to get the fat and ugly girl out of the way. Everyone, including the fat and ugly girl, was aware of this social maneuver. That was, after all, the only reason a fat and ugly girl bothered to be seen at a mixer with one of her gorgeous friends: to catch the crumbs.

The mixer was ten minutes old when I noticed Dolores Crosley. I knew that I needed someone to take care of her fat and ugly friend. But Gordon Feldameano was

97

busy talking to one of the chaperones. Gordon was that sort of guy. Tom Lanner, though a very nice person, did not want to dance with that fat and ugly girl.

"Hey, Tom," I said, "let's ask those two girls over there to dance."

"Where?"

"Those two, right there."

"Are you kidding?"

"No. Look, I'll ask the one on the left and you take. . . ."

"No way. Nooo way. Why don't I take the one on the left and you can have the other one."

"Look, Tom, I'd do it for you. Come on, just one dance."

"She really looks lousy."

"For Christ's sake, Lanner, I'm not asking you to marry her. I'm just asking you to dance with her."

"I don't know. Let me think about it for a while."

Just then I saw Gordon Feldameano, who was intently draining a Pepsi bottle into his mouth, walk away from the chaperone toward us. There was no one more brilliant than Gordon Feldameano for taking care of fat and ugly girls. Gordon had a soft spot in his head. He was a Christian.

Gordon Feldameano went to daily Mass and Holy Communion, never missed his morning and evening prayers, used part of his lunch time to say the rosary and, whenever he was there for a fair amount of time, meditated in the bathroom.

Gordon Feldameano excelled in amusing fat and ugly girls because he was so sincere. I had been tipped off by John Romans, Gordon's best friend, how to goad Gordon into action.

"Look, Gordon," I said as he approached Lanner and me, "see that girl over near the radiator? Why don't you ask her to dance?"

"No, I don't feel like it."

"I happen to know, Gordon, that she's a very pleasant person. I always see her at Saturday night novena. But just because she's a little overweight. . . ."

"A little overweight!" Gordon Feldameano exclaimed.

". . . All right," I conceded, "a lot overweight." I had momentarily forgotten that Gordon Feldameano's eyes weren't as dull as his mind. "Just because she's a lot overweight, she's going to have to stand there all night and suffer the social humiliation of having no one ask her to dance."

But even as I aimed Gordon Feldameano's emotions at that fat and ugly girl, I was beginning to feel apprehensive. Unlike others of her breed, the fat on her frame didn't hang in a very friendly fashion. Instead it stood like sheets of metal against her structure.

"She doesn't look like she's that nice of a person," said Gordon Feldameano.

"That's the problem," I countered. "Since she doesn't look like a nice person, everyone presumes that she isn't."

"I really don't feel much like dancing right now," he repeated.

"All right, Gordon, be that way. But do this for me. Just think about what would be the right thing to do."

Gordon Feldameano's morality button was in perfect operating order. Only a few seconds of silence passed before he quietly stated, "I'll do it."

Gordon and I waited for a slow song and, when it came, walked over to Dolores Crosley and her fat and ugly friend. I was already starting to dance with Dolores while Gordon was still in the process of introducing himself to the fat and ugly girl. If Gordon Feldameano stopped you on the street to ask you what time it was, he would first introduce himself.

"Good evening," he said, "my name is Gordon Feldameano. I attend Bremmer High School where I am presently a sophomore. I would like to know if you would be interested in dancing with. . . ."

Nothing moved on her but a slab of fat with five toes on it, better known as her right foot. It shot out from under her directly into Gordon Feldameano's left shin. Normally Christians demonstrate a high tolerance for pain. Gordon's stoicism, however, had been caught napping.

"Aaaaaah." Gordon grabbed his wounded shin with both hands while he tried to maintain his balance on one leg. He looked up at her disbelievingly. She put her hands on her hips and glared back at him. "What are you, a wise guy?"

Gordon Feldameano was still "aaaaahing" all over the place, but now his aaaaahings weren't nearly as loud as the first few. Nor were they as straight. The shock was beginning to wear off, allowing the "aaaaahings" to blend with low groans of agony.

When Gordon Feldameano had yelled out his initial announcement of pain, everybody in the basement turned around and stared at him. Like all true Christians, Gordon Feldameano detested being the object of attention; so there was nothing else he could do.

St. Bastion's school basement was extremely long and narrow. Everyone at the mixer was in one end of the basement where the record player and the soft-drinks tables were located. The chaperones, who made certain that all of us stayed directly beneath the glow of Commonwealth Edison, didn't bother lighting the rest of the basement. All you could see down that tunnel of black was the illuminated exit sign above the entrance doors to the basement. That was Gordon Feldameano's goal as he limped out of the yellow and into the dungeon darkness of St. Bastion's basement.

Although the slow song continued to play, no one danced as we all watched the progress of Gordon's shadow. In what seemed like an hour later, we finally saw the silhouette of Gordon Feldameano pass beneath the exit sign and through the door, still limping and still "aaaaahing."

Tom Lanner and I walked home from the mixer with Billy Palaglan, a guy we knew from the neighborhood. Palaglan had gone to the mixer by himself but had decided to walk home with Lanner and me since we all lived in the same direction.

"What do you think of Crosley, Tom?" I asked.

"She's nice looking, that's for sure."

"She may be nice looking," agreed Palaglan, "but she really knows it."

"Of course she knows it," I said. "That kind of thing is hard to keep a secret. What did you expect her parents to do, Palaglan, hide all the mirrors from the day she was born?"

"I'm entitled to my opinion, you know. I think she's very conceited."

"You're full of shit," I said.

"Up yours," he calmly replied.

Sometimes a "you're full of shit"-"up yours" exchange would almost demand a physical confrontation. But it

101

wasn't what you said that mattered but how you said it. If you said, "You're full of shit" very loudly and in a nasty way at someone, and he replied in an equally loud and nasty manner, "Up yours," then you would shortly find yourself in a fight. But Palaglan and I weren't yelling at one another. We were just talking very matter-of-factly, as if we were two television newsmen exchanging comments about something that had happened in the news.

A few days later I called up Dolores Crosley and asked her to go to the show with me on the following Saturday night. She accepted. During our phone conversation, she spoke three words: "Hello," "yes," and "good-bye."

We went to the Hillcrest Theater and saw a romance movie. It was lousy. There was nothing to it. I think that you should feel something after seeing a movie: happy, sad, mad, something. The only emotion I felt after viewing that film was gypped.

That night, though, it didn't matter. I didn't go to the Hillcrest Theater because I wanted to see a movie but because I wanted to take Dolores to a movie. There's a difference.

Neither of us said anything as we sat in the theater waiting for the show to begin. On the bus ride to the Hillcrest we had hardly talked, either. It was, after all, our first date so I wasn't expecting much conversation. Actually it was my first date with anyone so I didn't know what to expect.

About five minutes after the show began, I thought I'd put my arm around Dolores. And I thought about it for the next two-and-one-half hours. But I just couldn't get up enough nerve to do it.

At that age I didn't function well sexually unless I was in a crowd. When I went to parties where they played "Spin the Bottle" and stuff like that, I never had any problems. But when I was alone with a girl I just couldn't get going. If there had been nine or ten of my friends sitting around me at the show, playing a game called "Put Your Arm Around the Girl," then I wouldn't have had any problem. But there weren't, so I did.

First, I put my hand on the arm rest Dolores and I shared. Then I moved my hand up and scratched the back of my head for a while. I then slowly slid my elbow onto the back of my chair. But that was as far as I got.

I tried reasoning with myself. Look, the problem is that you're thinking too much about it. What you're going to do is silently count to ten and then, without thinking about it, you're going to put your arm around her.

I immediately counted to ten and did not put my arm around her. Again I silently counted to ten and again I didn't put my arm around Dolores. I tried counting backward but that also didn't work. I was sure getting to know my numbers but that was about it.

Perhaps, I decided, I was thinking too much about it as I counted to ten. I'd let the action of the movie determine for me when I'd make the move. That way it would be a reflex action. I wouldn't have time to worry about it.

The leading character was having dinner with his boss in some restaurant. The instant the movie changed to another scene, I'd put my arm around Dolores. I wouldn't even hesitate.

The leading lady walked in and sat down next to the

leading man. At that point in the film they weren't too crazy about each other. He started mocking her and, as he did so, he put his arm around her. She gave him a shocked stare and said very coolly, "That's a very personal thing to do to someone you hardly know."

That was it. There was no way that I was going to get my arm around Dolores now. I wasn't in a big rush to give her the impression that I was a sex maniac. If she spread something like that around the neighborhood, I was afraid that my first date would also be my last.

The restaurant scene was immediately followed by a "seat-slithering" scene. That's where the movie maker tries to shock the hell out of you by suddenly showing you something that's either very violent or sexy. In this case, it was a very sexy scene.

The leading man and the leading lady were in this apartment making out. They were really going after each other. Being a sophomore, I knew that I shouldn't be impressed by such a scene. But I still slithered down a little in my seat before I managed to regain my composure.

My eyes slid sideways to see Dolores' reaction. There was none. She sat there as if she were watching a Post Grape-Nuts commercial.

A few moments later Dolores casually shifted her weight in my direction, putting her back into the corner of the seat that was closest to me. I couldn't believe it. Obviously she wanted me to put my arm around her.

For the past half hour my elbow had been resting on the back of my seat. When my mind gave the command to my arm to throw itself around Dolores, it barely shuddered. I tried to move my fingers and felt only a tingling sensation. They were drowsy but they had not yet fallen asleep. The rest of the arm, however, was totally unconscious. It took me five minutes to drag it back down into my lap.

On the bus ride home Dolores again did not say anything. She didn't talk at the restaurant where we stopped for a hamburger and coke. On her front porch I said goodnight. She nodded. That was it.

When I got home that night I waited until the rest of the family was in bed. Then I went into the living room, sat on the couch, gazed out the front window, and wondered how soon it would be before someone stole Dolores Crosley away from me.

The living room was buried under a blanket of black even more intense than the night outside. Warm air from the lungs of the basement furnace whispered self-consciously along the walls. The living room clock, now devoid of human competition, yelled out obnoxiously with each tick. Every few minutes a car would slap down the street. Its wheels would skim along and rip open the edges of puddles left lingering in the curbs from an early evening rain.

After having just gone out with the most beautiful girl I had ever personally known, I knew that I'd never be able to hold on to her. Dolores might temporarily think that I was in her league, but how long could she remain so naive? I figured that within a week some six-foot, four-inch millionaire senior high school football player with a three thousand I.Q. would find out about Dolores Crosley and that would be the ball game.

As I sat there on the living room couch, staring out the window, the waves of worry breaking over my body began taking their toll. My stomach started feeling like someone was trying to hollow it out with an ice pick. The muscles in my legs were turning to Jell-O and I was getting a terrific headache.

It wasn't love or anything like that. More like I had just been given a twenty-pound box of Fannie May Chocolates and told that if I couldn't handle it, the box would be given to someone else. I love Fannie May Chocolates. I could eat a two-pound box within minutes. Even a five-pound box I could handle, if given sufficient time. But twenty pounds of Fannie May would be too much of a good thing. Dolores Crosley was pure Fannie May.

Every time I saw Dolores it was like our first date. We would both sit and say almost nothing. Not that I didn't try. For about a month I would occasionally stop by Dolores' house to see her. She would sit in a straight-back chair in one corner of her living room and I would sit in another straight-back chair in the opposite corner. No matter what I talked about or the questions I asked, I could get only four sounds to emit from Dolores' mouth: "yes," "no," "oh," and "I don't know." If I had told her I was going to burn her house down, pour concrete over her family, and throw her in front of a train, Dolores Crosley would have responded with "yes," "no," "oh," or "I don't know."

After numerous visits to Dolores' house and a few more dates with her. I decided that when that six-foot, four-inch millionaire senior high school football player with the three thousand I.Q. came along, he could have her.

Years later I ran into Dolores Crosley in downtown Chicago. Her four-word vocabulary had increased to the point that she could tell me she was working as a secretary at an advertising firm. Dolores' six-foot, four-inch millionaire senior high school football player with the three thousand I.Q. had finally come along. He worked as an accountant at the same firm. They were getting married in three weeks.

Although my voice wished her all the luck in the world, it was my mind that reserved it for him. No matter how good Dolores was in bed, sooner or later he'd have to get up.

In the middle of November Tom Lanner, Timmy Heidi, and I went to a Friday night mixer that was held in the basement of St. Basil's School, just north of my neighborhood.

I spent most of the night shooting the bull with the guys or dancing with different girls. It was a typical mixer except for the last three dances.

I saw her standing on the other side of the hall with three or four of her friends. From a distance she looked pretty good. As the sounds of a slow song began to wobble through the room, I walked over to her and asked her to dance. Up close she looked fantastic.

Although we held each other loosely and shuffled our feet slightly, we really didn't dance at all. We just stood there and talked. Somewhere during those dances she became as beautiful as Dolores Crosley, but in a different way. Not only was she as attractive as Dolores but, even better, she sounded as good as Dolores Crosley looked.

The lights were abruptly turned up even brighter than usual to indicate that the mixer was over. A line was beginning to form in front of the coat room. Someone was making an announcement over the public address system about the next mixer. One of her girlfriends was telling her that they had to leave now because so and so's father was outside already, waiting to pick them up.

"Thanks for the dances," I said.

"Thank you."

One of her friends tugged on her arm. "Come on, we've got to get going."

"It was nice talking to you," she said as she began putting on the coat and scarf her friend had brought her.

"It was nice talking to you, too."

By now she had, along with her girlfriend, become entangled among the people who were drifting toward the door.

"Are you coming here next week?" I yelled.

"No," she called back. "I already promised some of my friends that I would go with them to the dance over at St. Bruno's."

"Okay, then I'll see you there."

A few minutes later the school basement was nearly empty. I was putting on my coat when Heidi and Lanner came down the stairs looking for me.

"Where the hell have you been, Ryan?" Heidi asked. "We've been waiting outside for you."

"Sorry. I had trouble finding my coat."

Heidi and Lanner began talking about whether to stop for a snack at Gussie's Restaurant, but my mind was still mulling over those final moments with that girl. St. Bruno's parish was, by bus, about thirty-five minutes away from my neighborhood. I had some idea of where the school was, but I didn't know exactly how to get there. It was then that I realized I had forgotten to ask that girl her name. If I didn't go to the dance at St. Bruno's, I'd never see her again.

Stepping through the school doors into the bristling night air. "Hey," I said, "do either of you guys know where St. Bruno School is?"

"I do," said Timmy Heidi. "That's the neighborhood I grew up in."

"Really, you're not shittin' me?"

"Why would I do that?"

"I don't know. Hey, that's great. They're having a dance there next Friday night. You wanna go?"

"Aw, maybe."

"Come on, Heidi. I told some girl that I'd meet her there and I'm not too sure on how to get there."

"Yeah, why not. I'll go."

"How about you, Tom," I asked, "you wanna come along, too?"

"I'd like to," he said, "but I can't. I gotta work that Friday night."

"I thought you only worked a few hours after school at the food store," Heidi said.

"That's right," Tom replied. "But I got another job. You know that factory over on 116th and Pulaski?"

"You mean the one that makes school desks?" I asked.

"That's the one. I got a job there sweeping up the floor, taking out the garbage, and doing things like that on every other Friday night."

I knew why Lanner worked. He had to. But that night, I tried kidding him about it. "Man, Tom, with all that money you're making, you're gonna be a rich man when you grow up."

"Yeah," said Heidi, "if he has enough strength left to grow up."

During that week I must have imagined a million obstacles that were going to stop me from attending that St. Bruno mixer. My parents would get ticked off at me and wouldn't let me out. The paster of St. Bruno's would die and they'd call off the mixer. I'd break something, like my leg. I'd get the flu. Heidi would get the flu and I wouldn't be able to find the place. But when Friday night came strolling in, I was ready.

That evening I walked over to Timmy Heidi's house wearing my best sport coat and tie. Only a few hours earlier both of them had been revitalized at the dry cleaners. My chest was bottled in the only cuff-link shirt I owned. I had even bothered to shine my shoes and I was never a strong believer in that. The way I figured it, if some girl bothered to look at my shoes long enough to realize they were dirty, it meant that either she preferred to look at my shoes rather than me or she was a *neat* freak. Either way she wouldn't be of much use to me, so there was no point in shining my shoes for her. But that night I was taking no chances.

As Timmy Heidi came out of his house, I could see that beneath his topcoat he was wearing his usual sport coat and tie. As we walked toward the bus stop Heidi started sniffing. "Hey, Ryan, did you take a bubble bath tonight?"

"Knock it off, Heidi. I'm wearing some of my father's after-shave."

"That broad you're meeting must really be something."

"You mean, 'girl,' don't you?"

"Oh, my deepest apologies, sir," Heidi said in pseudo-seriousness. "Please understand that it was only an innocent slip of the tongue. I in no way intended to offend your high standards. . . ."

"You know, Heidi, sometimes, you're a real pain in the ass."

He just laughed at me.

Thirty-five minutes later we were getting off the bus at 79th and Halsted. It was a quarter after seven. The dance at St. Bruno's wouldn't begin until eight o'clock.

"Let's stop in that restaurant over there," said Heidi, "and have a Coke and kill some time. I'm pretty sure that St. Bruno's is only about three blocks from here."

"Pretty sure? I thought you knew."

"Don't worry about it. Remember, I grew up in this neighborhood."

A half hour later Heidi and I left the restaurant, walked a block over and three blocks down. But there was no St. Bruno School.

"I know where I made my mistake," said Heidi. "It's three blocks from the other side of Halsted, not this side."

"I know where I made my mistake," I said. "Let's get moving; it's starting to get late."

"Relax," said Heidi, "we've got plenty of time."

Six blocks later we had a lot less of it, and still no St. Bruno's. I was beginning to panic. It was almost nine o'clock.

"For God's sake, Heidi, I thought you grew up in this neighborhood?"

"I did. I just can't understand it."

"Are you positive you've got the right neighborhood?"

"Very funny."

"I'm not trying to be funny. All I want to do is get to St. Bruno's and fast."

"I tell you what," said Heidi. "I'll go up to one of these houses and ask somebody where St. Bruno's is."

"Just do it fast, will ya?"

An old lady answered at the first house he tried. She huddled in the doorway for at least five minutes talking and gesturing to Heidi. Finally, he came away from the door and returned to the sidewalk.

"What the hell took you so long?"

"She doesn't speak very good English," Heidi said. "I had trouble understanding her. According to her, St. Bruno's is about ten blocks from here. It's almost on Ashland Avenue. That's certainly not the way I remember it."

"I know, I know, you grew up in this neighborhood."

"I did."

"Look, Heidi, that dance is almost half over by now. If we don't trot the whole ten blocks, it's going to be finished by the time we get there."

Heidi buttoned up his topcoat so that it wouldn't flop around. "Ready when you are."

After ten blocks of running, interrupted only briefly by two rapid-walking rest periods, Timmy Heidi and I found ourselves standing in front of Bruno's Pizzeria, which was closed for remodeling.

It was too late now. I could tell that Heidi felt as lousy as I did, if that was possible.

"I'm sorry, Eddie," he said. "I can't understand it."

"That's all right. I mean, you didn't plan on things turning out this way. That's the way life goes sometimes. Don't worry about it."

I could have killed him.

Walking down the street, looking for a bus stop. "I

can't understand it," Heidi said. "I grew up in this neighborhood."

"Can I ask you something, Heidi?"

"Sure. Anything."

"How old were you when your family moved out?"

"Four."

Cross-country sounds like the name of a travelogue or the answer to "Where are you going?" It certainly doesn't sound like the name of a sport, which it is.

In cross-crountry there are no balls thrown, caught, kicked, hit at, or put through a hoop. There are no touchdowns, tackles, home runs, stolen bases, or shots on goal. Cross-country offers little but human speed and not much of it at that. In a society where even old ladies regularly fly at better than three hundred miles an hour, watching some skinny high school kid trot through a forest preserve in what looks like his underwear is no big thrill, unless you happen to be somewhat strange to begin with.

Cross-country consists of running two miles, three miles, or whatever number of miles is customary for that particular race, over the lousiest land you can find. For urban schools, such land may be city streets.

When two schools hold a cross-country meet, be they high schools or colleges, each school usually brings along as many runners as it wants. The first five runners from each school to cross the finish line receive a certain number of points. For instance, if a runner places third in the race, he gets three points. The school with the

115

lowest number of total points wins. Exciting. Sometimes a number of schools will get together and hold a cross-country meet. The ensuing race looks like a moving riot.

Most cross-country runners are notorious losers in the lottery of life. They're bad students, have pimple personalities, usually weigh less than five pounds, and stink in every other sport. Not surprising that the average cross-country runner has a strong desire to run as fast and as far as possible.

Although an individual has to have a certain amount of raw ability to be a great cross-country runner, just about anybody, if he runs long enough and often enough, can be a good one. All he needs is a head of solid determination undiluted by an ounce of either talent or intelligence. People who have such assets play sports that make sense, such as football.

Football gets you glory. Score a touchdown and thousands of people stand up and cheer you, girls in short skirts kick up their legs, and all of your teammates pat you on the ass and tell you what a great guy you are.

In cross-country, the only ones to greet you at the finish line are your coach with a stopwatch, who yells out your time, and a few of your teammates who ask you where the hell you've been.

Football, like most other sports, has a future. If you're exceptionally good at it, when you get out of school you can play pro ball, make a lot of money, and get even more glory.

If you're a cross-country runner, once you leave school the only way you're going to make practical use of your ability is if you become either a purse snatcher or the world's fastest mailman.

Football fanatics will tell you that football players

deserve all the glory they get because football is such a rough sport that you can even get killed playing it. True, but it rarely occurs. About the worst thing that can normally happen to a football player is that he gets his leg broken. Even if he does, he can stand on the sidelines during the game, lean on his crutches, and soak up sympathy from the crowd.

Cross-country runners can also get killed participating in their sport, especially if they try to cross against the light.

In a cross-country race, the real action goes on between the runner's ears. He spends the first few minutes of the race telling himself that he's going to cover all the distance ahead of him in a few dozen giant steps. Minutes later the muscles in his legs are knotting up and turning into rocks while his stomach is curling up toward his Adam's apple. His throat has nearly swollen shut. Only a slice of it remains open for his breath to squeeze through. As he listens to the air in his lungs trying to yank itself free and feels the salt from his sweat reaming out his eyes, he asks himself repeatedly how he could have allowed himself to become involved in something so asinine as cross-country.

Not long after, his personal pep talk begins. He tells his legs that they never felt stronger even though they're now feeling nothing at all. He forces his chest to reach out even farther for the incoming oxygen. Wiggling his head in an attempt to shake his eyes free from the sweat, he tells himself that he can do it, he can do it, he can do it.

When he is within a couple of hundred yards of the finish line, he goes into his "kick," a cross-country runner's term that means nothing more than putting the accelerator all the way down to the floor, so that when the body crosses the finish line it has not even a whim of energy left.

Ten minutes later he is still breathing heavily as he tries to coax his body back into reality, to recover from the beating it has just undergone. And he is smiling because, once again, he has proven to that most important audience of all—himself—that he's still one tough bastard.

Being on a cross-country team is like belonging to an S/M club. Cross-country produces the kind of guy who, even though he hates it, will eat the crust and throw away the rest of the bread. A good cross-country runner loves doing what he hates.

At Bremmer High School no one ever had to "try out" for the cross-country team. Brother Well, the former boxer, was the coach. If you came out to all the practices and ran your ass off—and Brother Well seemed to know instinctively if you were, indeed, running your ass off—then you were on the team.

The cross-country season began in September, at the beginning of the school year, and ended in mid-November. Each day during the season the members of the Bremmer cross-country team would meet behind the school on the athletic field. Brother Well would lead off the practice session by having the members of the team say a "Hail Mary" together. But silently each runner prayed his own prayer: "Dear God, make me into a football player." The team would do some calisthenics and then begin its two-mile run, which would carry the runners across the athletic field and down one of the residential streets that bordered the school. Everyone ran this two-mile jaunt twice each afternoon.

All cross-country runners have the same physical build; that is, almost none at all. When the typical cross-country team stands up at the starting line, it looks like a picket fence. During the first few weeks of practice, however, there are a couple of exceptions. Inevitably two fat guys, housed in gray flannel sweat suits, come out to practice with the announced intention of running and sweating off their excess weight. When the team runs its miles, the two overweight guys chug along blocks behind. The gray flannel sweat suits become drenched with perspiration, their faces turn orange from effort and the foreheads wring so tight with tension that it appears as if both of them are on the verge of having a hernia. Each day the two fat guys lag farther behind. After a few weeks one of them topples over and the other guy eats him.

One year the two fat guys who joined the Bremmer cross-country team were Howard Flatzer, a junior, and George Gelley, who was a senior. "Fat" really isn't an accurate description of them because both Howard and George were quite muscular. It was just that their stomachs were buried beneath a few inches of shaky fat.

Howard Flatzer only came out for three days. His family doctor discovered what he was doing and told Howard that he should have himself committed. Howard, it seems, was a severe asthmatic.

If it had been any sport other than cross-country, the coach would have noticed immediately that there was something wrong with Howard Flatzer. Every time Howard ran more than twenty feet without taking a break, he'd faint. But in cross-country, such a reaction isn't unusual for any overweight kid who tries to move both legs simultaneously.

That left only George Gelley to rumble behind the rest of the cross-country team. George Gelley was his legal name but his real name was Bippo. It was one of those nicknames that so perfectly described its bearer that, if it hadn't been for report cards, class attendance sheets, and other legal paraphernalia, Bippo, along with the rest of us, would have forgotten who George Gelley was.

Bippo had the body of a six-foot, four-inch man that had been compressed into a five-foot, one-inch frame. He had a flower head that was constantly in full bloom, a neck that appeared to be made out of eighteen-inch cable, and such big feet that when he followed the cross-country team through the streets, he had to wait for an intersection before he could change directions. When God had poured the strength into Bippo, someone forgot to say "when." His arms and legs literally bulged from the mountains of muscle that smothered beneath his skin.

Bippo's mother had deserted the family shortly after his younger brother, Donald, was born. Bippo never admitted, though, that his mother had cut out. He told everyone that she worked for the telephone company. When some of his friends asked why they never saw her around the house, he told them that she worked all three shifts.

Bippo's father, George Senior, as he insisted on being called, was an alcoholic and a tree trimmer, in that order. Wherever George Senior worked he drew a crowd. He had a habit of falling out of his work. Much to the disappointment of the crowd, however, he never hurt himself. Because of the lubricating effects of his drinking diet, George Senior usually hit the ground like a rag doll. Only once, when George Senior got careless and put a bottle of wine in his back pocket just before the fall, did he suffer a substantial injury. He spent the next four days picking "Mogen David" out of his ass.

Besides being an alcoholic, George Senior was also a tough guy. One night two cops, driving by in a squad car, heard shots being fired in a corner tavern. They jumped out of their car and ran to the front door, only to meet George Senior coming out of the tavern with a shot gun in his hand.

One of the cops grabbed George Senior from behind, put a choke hold on him, and began applying pressure. The other cop started swinging his night stick into George Senior's forehead. Either maneuver should have knocked him out in a couple of seconds. But three minutes later, as the two amazed cops continued to choke and batter, George Senior was still awake and eager to continue on his way.

After a few more minutes George Senior quit struggling. "Okay," he said, "I've had enough." One of the cops handcuffed him and began leading him to the squad car.

"Wait a minute, fellas," said George Senior, "I think you better take me to the hospital first."

"Why?" asked one of the cops. "You don't appear to be injured."

"Lift up my shirt," said George Senior. The cop did. George Senior had three bullet holes in his stomach. George Senior wasn't the one who had been doing the shooting. He was the guy they had been shooting at.

Donald, Bippo's younger brother, was a nice enough kid but he was terrified of everything in existence. It had taken Donald the first five years of his life just to get up enough courage to learn how to walk. That was how Bippo got his name.

Until Donald decided to walk, he was carried everywhere he wanted to go by Bippo. Many kids thought that was funny. Occasionally some kid would think it was too funny. Bippo would then set Donald down and promptly punch out the kid. In doing so, Bippo would hit the kid with two quick shots, one from each fist. The first fist, landing in the stomach, would make a "bip" sound, which would be followed instantaneously by the impact of the second fist, "po," as it dented the kid's forehead. Bippo, being the size that he was, had to first double a guy over before he could hit him in the head.

When the cross-country team made its two-mile runs each day, it would start at the eastern corner of the Bremmer athletic field and patter across it before entering the streets of the adjoining neighborhood. Most of the athletic field was reserved for the varsity football team. The cross-country runners limited their intrusion to running along the borders of the reserved area. Since the football players had much more space than they needed, they hardly noticed when the cross-country runners strung by. Until the day that Bippo bored through.

The cross-country runners were getting ready for the second of their two-mile runs. Most of them were limbering up by walking around inside the small plot of athletic field that had been allotted to them. Bippo decided to start running a few minutes before the coach was scheduled to call the team up to the starting line. Bippo often did this so that he might finish on the same day as the rest of the runners.

A few of his fellow teammates watched Bippo inch across the football practice field and wondered why he hadn't yet traded in his gray-flannel sweat suit for a cheeseburger. They saw a missed pass fall in front of Bippo's feet. Maybe he saw it, maybe he didn't. Regardless, Bippo's four-inch stride brought his massive foot into the side of the football, sending it skipping across the field.

The player who had missed the pass thought that Bippo was being a wise guy. He ran up to Bippo and told him so. Bippo's feet never missed a stride as the hands dispatched the football player. BIPPO.

Another football player, seeing what had happened, ran up behind Bippo and made a perfect diving tackle. The football player must have thought he had hit a statue. Bippo's body hardly flinched from the collision. Being built the way he was, Bippo's level of gravity was approximately an inch above his ankles. He just kept shuffling along, dragging behind him the football player who still clung to Bippo's leg.

A second player ran up behind Bippo and pounced on his shoulders. From the front two more dug into him.

A few of the cross-country runners had started to go toward Bippo to give him some help, but Brother Well told them to stay put. Knowing the mentality of cross-country runners, Brother Well knew that wanting to help out Bippo wasn't their primary motive. Cross-country runners love to suffer. What better way to enjoy yourself than by having some football player tear you apart.

From where the cross-country team stood, Bippo could no longer be seen. He was obliterated completely by a pile of football players, a pile that was almost imperceptibly, yet definitely, moving.

The head football coach, Nick Venuti, had been passively watching his players trying to bury Bippo. Venuti stood there with his bloated chest and eight-foot arms with the elbows hovering around the knees, twirling his whistle chain around his finger, reversing the spin when he ran out of chain. Somewhere that whistle was always on Coach Venuti; hanging around his neck, wrapped in his fist, twirling around his finger, or stuck in his mouth. The reason was obvious. Coach Venuti whistled better than he talked.

Finally Coach Venuti stuck the whistle in his mouth. His breath took a few steps back, in order to get some running distance, and then raced forward through the whistle. The resulting shrill shrieked across the athletic field. Upon hearing it the football players peeled off of Bippo and trotted back to join the rest of the team. Bippo, who hadn't lost a stride throughout the attack, hardly seemed to notice that he was no longer carrying four other people along with him.

Coach Venuti ran over to Bippo and said something to him. The cross-country team, still watching, knew that Venuti was saying something unusual to Bippo. If he hadn't been, the coach would have whistled the message. Bippo listened and nodded in agreement. Coach Venuti finished talking and then jogged back to his waiting team.

Bippo, who had not stopped moving even to listen to Coach Venuti, continued to plop his feet across the rest of the athletic field and out onto the city streets. A few hours later, when Bippo came in from his two-mile run, the cross-country team got the news. Bippo was now a member of the Bremmer varsity football team.

In its sixteen years of existence Bremmer High School had never had a decent football team. Every season the team would manage to lose considerably more games than it won. With a student body of sixteen hundred students to choose from, Coach Venuti always came up with forty good football players. Together, however, they always made up one bad team. Almost every player that Coach Venuti chose had a blank space above his belt. No guts.

The problem was that Coach Venuti picked players because they were big and strong and not because they displayed any intense desire to play football. The players were aware of why they had been chosen for the team so they never bothered to hustle. The only way, for example, that a first-string player was going to lose his position to another guy on the team was if that guy suddenly grew stronger and bigger than the first-stringer was. So if you really wanted to play first-string football for Bremmer High School, instead of learning to throw a football better or tackle harder you would have been smarter to have gone out and bought some weights and a rack.

It wasn't difficult to spot Bippo on the football practice field that first day. He was the one who stood as tall as everyone else's elbow. The coach tried Bippo out at fullback. Every time Bippo carried the ball, it took seven guys to put him down. Coach Venuti was so thrilled with Bippo's performance that, during a five-minute break, he tried to hold a conversation with him. This was highly unusual for the coach because he didn't believe in fraternizing with his players. When Coach Venuti went to the zoo, he never fed the animals.

"Hey, Bippo, who do ya' think's gonna win the N.F.L. championship this year?"

Bippo was sitting on the ground, using a stick to pry

the mud out of his cleats. "I don't know. I don't follow professional sports."

"You don't what?"

"I don't follow professional sports. I don't cheer for General Motors, either."

"General Motors? What the hell has that got to do with anything? Come on, who do ya' think's gonna win the N.F.L. championship?"

"The Packers."

"Yeah, that's what I think, too."

Rain started dribbling from the sky. Bippo got up and began trotting toward the locker room, which stuck out from the southeastern wing of the school.

Coach Venuti sprang to his feet. "Where the hell are you going?"

"In."

"Why?"

"It's raining on me."

"So what?"

Bippo stopped running, turned around, and looked at Coach Venuti. "I get depressed when it rains on me."

"So what?"

Bippo began again to run toward the locker room. Coach Venuti blew hard on his whistle, but Bippo kept on moving.

Bippo continued to come to football practice, but only on the days it wasn't raining. With forty other players to keep Coach Venuti occupied, it didn't take him long to forget about a sarcastic dwarf who was afraid of the rain.

Two weeks after Bippo joined the football team Bremmer was scheduled to play its perennial patsy, St. Beatrice High School. Of the nine high schools that belonged to the Chicago Catholic Football Conference, St. Beatrice was the only one that had a completely black student enrollment. It was located in one of Chicago's worst inner-city ghettos. The other eight schools each had one head football coach and two or three assistants. St. Beatrice had one coach, and he only held practice three days a week. On the other two days he worked at a shoe store.

St. Beatrice was not only the blackest school in the Catholic Football Conference, it was also the smallest with 475 students. St. Edward's, the next smallest school, had over twice that many.

In addition to being the blackest and smallest, St. Beatrice was also the weakest. It was the only coeducational school in the conference. Only fifty-five of its students were boys. Bremmer had almost as many guys on its football team as St. Beatrice had in its entire school. St. Beatrice's football roster listed seventeen players.

Although Bremmer was supposedly a Catholic high school, its true religion was football. On Friday afternoons before the games, which were played on Sunday, the school would hold Mass in the gym, in the form of a football rally. Rallies weren't held for every game, but only for special ones, such as the homecoming game, and the ones we knew we'd win. There was always a rally held when we were scheduled to play St. Beatrice.

That year on the Friday afternoon before the St. Beatrice game, the last two classes of the day were canceled and all of us were packed onto the gym's wooden roll-away bleachers and folding chairs. The football players were sitting on the stage, trying to look terrifically humble about the whole thing. With their heads slightly bowed, they constantly exchanged shy little grins among themselves. They were a cute bunch. They really were. Bippo, sitting in the last row, could hardly be seen.

The student body spent the next two hours ranting such traditional war chants as "Hey, hey, what do you say, give that ball a fight . . ." and "Block that kick, hey, block that kick . . ." and "DEfense, DEfense, DEfense. . . ." A few of the school-spirit nuts, standing in front of the stage, led us through the cheers.

Unlike other Catholic boys' high schools, Bremmer didn't import female cheerleaders from the neighboring Catholic girls' school. Brother Purity probably presumed that if he did, with the kind of team we had no one would have bothered to watch the game.

In between chants different members of the team stood before the microphone, which was placed at the front of the stage, and attempted to further glorify the gallantry of the other thirty-nine goons sitting behind them.

Ed Frick, one of the team's co-captain's, was the first to growl. "Well . . . guys, . . . all . . . I . . . know . . . is . . . we . . . worked . . . awful . . . hard . . . this . . . week . . . in . . . practice . . . and . . . let . . . me . . . tell . . . you, . . . we're . . . ready . . . for . . . them. . . ." It was the first time that anyone heard Ed Frick say more than three words without one of them being obscene.

All sixteen hundred of us cheered like mad. It wasn't that we were that impressed with what Ed Frick had said, it was simply a case of stimulus-reponse. Most people behave the way they're expected to behave and at football rallies we were expected to cheer. No matter what happened at those rallies, we cheered it. Every

128

word delivered over the microphone was greeted with wild enthusiasm. When one of the football players knocked over the microphone, that was cheered. If a teacher had chosen a football rally to drop dead at, we probably would have cheered that, too. If it was the right teacher he might have received a standing ovation.

The next guy to speak was Earl Benninger, the other co-captain. Earl was not your ordinary football player. There wasn't a thing in life worth possessing that Earl didn't already have. His family was extremely wealthy. He was good looking and smart, he was a great athlete, and he could play seventeen different musical instruments, all at the same time. Worst of all, Earl Benninger had such a pleasant personality that it was impossible for anyone, including myself, to dislike him. Earl Benninger was a very depressing person to be around.

As he stepped to the microphone to throw out some propaganda about the upcoming game, I thought to myself that it would have been nice to trade places with Earl. I've always been afflicted with a bad case of the-grass-looks-greener-on-the-other-side-of-the-fence complex. I'm even that way with myself. Yesterday looks better to me simply because there's a today. I know that's a dumb way to think. But just because you know that something you do is dumb, that doesn't necessarily mean you can stop doing it.

Less than a year after the day that he appeared on that stage, Earl got some girl pregnant and, like any fine young man would do, blew his life by dropping out of school and marrying her. He followed that up six weeks later by getting himself killed when his car slid under the back end of a trailer truck. All of this, of course, didn't cure me of my "grass is greener" complex. It just removed one yard from my view.

Earl Benninger said pretty much the same thing that Ed Frick did except that Earl talked like a human being. He told us how hard everyone on the team had worked in practice during the past week and how badly they wanted to win this game. Earl Benninger concluded by saying, "Believe me, fellows, . . ." (Earl was the type that always said "fellows," rather than "guys," "boys," or "shitheads") ". . . . we're going to give them everything we've got." Earl Benninger did not explain why St. Beatrice wanted forty cases of venereal disease.

Coach Venuti followed Earl Benninger to the microphone. As the coach lumbered up to the front of the stage, he momentarily went a little too far, bumping into the microphone stand. The pole on the stand slowly slid down until the microphone pointed directly at his navel. As Coach Venuti cleared his throat to speak, everyone in the gym heard a subway train rumble through his stomach. Naturally it got a big cheer.

"I'm not promising victory, men," the coach said, "but I'll tell you one thing. When that final whistle blows on Sunday afternoon, St. Beatrice is going to know it was in a football game." An avalanche of applause followed.

Coach Venuti smiled and tugged at his crotch. Onstage crotch tugging was a Coach Venuti trademark. When Jack Benny did well before an audience, he would take off his glasses and place them in his pocket. When Coach Venuti enjoyed the same kind of success, he would tug at his crotch.

The final words of the football rally were spoken by Brother Purity. "Boys, I know that you, as fine young Christian men, are going to pray to God that Bremmer

scores a great victory over St. Beatrice on Sunday."
Brother Purity proceeded to lead us in prayer and most
of us actually prayed, for what are gods for if not to win
football games?

Then came the grand finale. The football players
trotted out of the gym, dogging it as usual, and we
stood and sang the school song. No one at Bremmer
knew all the words. We didn't get many opportunities to
learn them. Outside of football rallies, the only times we
sang the school song were at football games when we
scored a touchdown.

The opposing stands at the Bremmer-St. Beatrice
game looked like the "before" and "after" pictures of a
football famine. The Bremmer bleachers were stuffed
with a few thousand fans, fat with smugness. Colorful
banners floated over their heads while soft drink and
peanut vendors zigzagged through the aisles. In the center of the crowd sat the fifty-piece Bremmer High
School band. Twenty male cheerleaders kept the mob
shouting.

On the other side of the field, the tiers of empty
stands were stained by only one spot of humanity, which
was composed of a few dozen St. Beatrice fans, two
skinny cheerleaders, one banner, no vendors, no hope,
and one kid with a bugle who had apparently decided
that he was going to use the time allotted to the football
game to learn how to play it.

As the forty Bremmer football players burst out of the
tunnel that led from the locker room, you could see that
their emotions were already on the rampage. They were
slapping each others' helmets, butting shoulders together,
and bouncing blocks into one another. The Bremmer
players were working harder in the warm-up against

each other than they had against their opponents in all the previous games.

The seventeen black football players who made up the St. Beatrice team followed the Bremmer mob out of the tunnel. The St. Beatrice boys looked like the clean-up crew for an all-night New Year's Eve party. Helmets held limply in their hands, they looked up at the thousands of Bremmer fans and saw the thumbs, all pointing down.

The final score was Bremmer: 40, St. Beatrice: 6. In the last minutes of the game St. Beatrice recovered a fumble at the Bremmer nine-yard line and ran it in for a touchdown. Watching Coach Venuti become enraged on the sidelines over the St. Beatrice touchdown, you realized that somewhere in his family tree there had to be Nero.

Every member of the Bremmer team got a chance to participate in the massacre except Bippo. A few days before the game Coach Venuti discovered what everybody else in the school already knew. Bippo was a boozer. At practice one of the assistant coaches had noticed that Bippo had alcohol on his breath.

"Hey, Bippo," said the assistant coach, "what's that I smell on your breath?"

"Toothpaste?" Bippo made the mistake of asking instead of telling.

"What did you brush your teeth with? Bourbon?"

According to the rules of the athletic department, any football player who drank alcohol was to be immediately suspended from the team. In reality, however, as long as you drank at the proper time and in the manner befitting a high school football player, you didn't get into trouble. Coach Venuti felt it was almost sacred tradition that high school football players drank beer and got drunk on weekends.

But Bippo was something else again. He drank constantly and was on the hard stuff besides. His father being a devout alcoholic, booze was about the only liquid refreshment that was kept in the house. Even though Bippo drank constantly his behavior never seemed to be affected by it, which meant that he was either always sober or always drunk.

Coach Venuti didn't like the idea of one of his players habitually guzzling hard liquor. He took it as an indication that Bippo was trying to usurp his and the assistant coaches' authority by drinking like them. If there was one thing Coach Venuti had less use for than a sarcastic dwarf who was afraid of the rain, it was an alcoholic sarcastic dwarf who was afraid of the rain.

The last game of the season, Bremmer's homecoming game, was considered the most important one. Losing your homecoming game was always a bit more painful than other losses. Bremmer's record was pure masochism. In its sixteen years of football it had never won its homecoming game.

That year's game was to be played against St. Francis High School. Since Bremmer and St. Francis recruited their students from basically the same neighborhoods, the rivalry between them was intense. Going into the Bremmer homecoming game, St. Francis had won all seven of its previous games. Only Bremmer stood between it and a perfect season.

The rumor was that if Bremmer managed to lose its homecoming game again, it would in the following season stoop to the lowest depths of depravity. It would schedule its homecoming game against St. Beatrice.

133

The word was also out that Brother Purity, the fathers club, and the alumni association, who together controlled the football program, had become fed up with the annual entree of humiliation served up at every homecoming game. If Coach Venuti, who had been the head football coach at Bremmer for the past eight years, lost his ninth straight homecoming game, he would probably have to start looking for another locker room to hang around in.

Homecoming weekend was a big deal at Bremmer. The rally would take place on Friday afternoon. On Saturday night the homecoming dance would be held in both the cafeteria and the gym, with a band in each one. On Sunday afternoon, of course, the homecoming game was played. After the game, at around five o'clock, a victory sock hop would be held in the gym even if Bremmer didn't win.

At the homecoming dance you discovered who among your fellow students was into bestiality. Surprisingly, the football players, despite their heavy social credentials, which should have enabled them to date the most attractive girls available, always brought dates that looked like themselves. The only difference between some of the football players and their girlfriends was that the girls had breasts and longer hair. Sometimes.

On the Sunday afternoon of that homecoming game, both sides of the field were swollen with fans. Even the fenced areas behind the end zones were stacked with spectators. At the end of the first half the score was tied at 14 all. But by the end of the third quarter, the score looked like the Bremmer team had forgotten to come out of the locker room after half time. It was 31 to 14 in favor of St. Francis High School.

By the middle of the fourth quarter it was 39 to 14. With the clarity that's characteristic of dying men, Coach Venuti started sending in his second- and third-string players, especially the seniors since it was the last game of their high school careers. With less than three minutes left in the game, Coach Venuti even decided to send in Bippo. Why not? he figured. There wasn't a cloud in the sky.

Bippo went in to play left defensive tackle, a position he had never played before. The ball was on the St. Francis thirty-yard line. On the first play Bippo pushed two linemen aside as if they were old ladies waiting at a bus stop and leveled the quarterback, who hadn't even straightened up from the snap. Bippo's tackle popped the ball out of the quarterback's hands. Bippo scooped it up. There were only twenty-five yards of open space between Bippo and a touchdown. He stuck the ball in against his belly and tied it in place with his wrap-around arms. Bippo then casually proceeded to drop one foot in front of the other.

"RUN RUN RUN." The thousands of Bremmer fans were yelling at him. They couldn't believe the paralyzing pace at which Bippo was moving. By the time he crossed the goal line, seven St. Francis players were hanging on him. A few seconds later Bippo rammed the ball into the end zone for the two-point conversion and the score was now St. Francis: 39, Bremmer: 22.

Bremmer made an onside kick and Bippo recovered it. On the first play Bippo carried the ball for a nine-yard gain. Two players were injured, not among the six that it took to bring him down, but the two that he fell on. In four out of the next five plays, Bippo carried the ball, his stumpy legs barging forward as if someone had told them there was booze buried in the end zone. Ninety seconds after Bippo scored his first touchdown for Bremmer High School, he scored his second one. Again he made the two-point conversion and the score now read St. Francis: 39, Bremmer: 30.

With only seven seconds left in the game, St. Francis, deep in its own territory, tried to punt the ball out. A Bremmer player blocked the kick and Bippo recovered the ball. One play later he scored his third touchdown and, a few seconds after that, followed it up with another two-point conversion. But time had run out. The final score was St. Francis: 39, Bippo: 38.

As Bippo was dissecting the St. Francis football team, the Bremmer fans—especially the members of the fathers club and the alumni association—were scanning their programs, looking for his number and trying to figure out who he was. If a player's jersey number wasn't listed in the program it usually meant that he was a sophomore who had, sometime during the season, been brought up from the sophomore football team to join the varsity. Since the programs were printed before the season began, these new sophomore players weren't listed on the official roster. But because Bippo had also joined the team midway through the season, he wasn't listed either, even though he was a senior.

When they couldn't find his number in the program, the members of the fathers club and the alumni association presumed that Bippo was a sophomore sensation who would be around for two more full seasons. Before the homecoming game even ended, visions of a Bremmer football dynasty danced in their heads.

When the truth of the situation began spreading a few hours later, the officers of the fathers club, the alumni association, and even Brother Purity himself went to Coach Venuti and asked him how he could have overlooked such talent for so long. Three days later the coach gave him his reply in the form of a letter of resignation. I don't know if the story about it having been written in crayon was true or not. Part of the letter did say something about another player having to run alongside Bippo and hold an umbrella over Bippo's head if he was to realize his full potential as a football player.

The victory sock hop, held that night in the school gym, was saturated with people celebrating the one-point loss. The guys who were there had attended the game but most of the girls couldn't have been less interested. One overdeveloped girl, whose breasts had obviously siphoned off some of the cells destined for her brain, kept asking everyone she met, "Who won? Who won?"

It was customary that at the victory sock hop, the homecoming queen would give the game ball to the outstanding player of the game. When the sock hop was half over, the record music would be stopped and Brother Purity would announce over the public address system that, onstage, the homecoming queen was about to present the game ball to the day's outstanding football player.

Usually everyone would just keep talking and making noise. A few girls would even continue to dance. Brother Purity would stand at the microphone for a few moments, waiting for silence. Then he would say, "Well, that's better," even though it wasn't, and the presentation would take place with only those who were involved being aware of it. But that year, everybody saw it.

The proper people were beginning to gather on stage. Brother Purity, the officers of the fathers club and the alumni association, Coach Venuti, and some local politicians. The usual collection of carcasses for such an event.

Brother Purity told Bippo, who was to receive the award, to stand in the center of the stage. Then Brother Purity took the homecoming queen gently by the arm and led her over next to Bippo. The presentation was still at least five minutes away because Brother Purity hadn't yet made his announcement over the public address system. After taking care of the homecoming queen and Bippo, Brother Purity scampered among the dignitaries, suggesting to each where they should stand for the presentation.

Annie Crachshantz was a typical Bremmer homecoming queen. They all looked the same. Like Coach Venuti's older brother. Every year ten or fifteen girls would be nominated by their boyfriends, who just happened to be football players, for homecoming queen. Five-foot-square posters with tiny snapshots in the center would appear throughout the school. The girl who had the boyfriend with the most hustle and friends won. Every year the ugliest nominee had the most ambitious boyfriend.

Brother Purity, standing at the edge of the stage, was beginning to make his announcement over the public address system. A few feet behind him stood Bippo, Annie Crachshantz, and the herd of dignitaries.

"You're awful short for a football player," said Annie Crachshantz as she looked down at Bippo.

"You're awful ugly for a homecoming queen," he replied.

138

"Oh, so you're one of those guys."

"What do you mean?"

"You know what I mean. You're one of those guys who thinks that just because he's talking to a female, he can treat her like dirt. You think that just because you're a male, you're superior to all women."

Brother Purity was at that part of his announcement where he was standing silently in front of the microphone, waiting for the crowd noise to disappear.

"So you think I should treat you just like another guy?" Bippo asked.

"That's right, shorty."

BIPPO.

The mob went mute at the sight of their homecoming queen being punched out. On stage, huge caverns appeared on the faces of everybody where the lips had previously been. Brother Purity, still unaware of what had just happened behind him, made the comment he always made after waiting a few moments for silence.

"Well, that's better."

8

Una was a girl who loved old people, little kids, folk music, girl scouting, sewing, baking, playing "Tammy" on the piano, long dresses, extracurricular activities, bike riding, God, and the Fourth of July. She loved sunrises, sunsets, and almost everything in between, except me.

On a night in early spring, when the earth, still defrosting from winter, squished like sponge under one's feet and the sky constantly cried for summer, I met Una.

Directly across the street from the park in my neighborhood was a custard stand, which was rimmed by a five-foot eave. After supper Paul Zeppl and I had gone to the park to "hit 'em out" for a while. Bouquets of clouds containing various shades of gray sagged in the sky. We had only played for about twenty minutes when we heard a hiss sizzling across the field toward us. A familiar voice to anyone who played as much baseball in the spring as Paul Zeppl and I did. A wall of rain was streaking across the park.

Paul and I scooped up our shoes, jackets, the bats, gloves and baseball and started running for the custard stand, which waited a few hundred yards away on the other side of 111th Street. Within seconds sheets of water lashed past us. By the time we got under the protection of the custard-stand eave, every pore on our bodies had been riveted by rain.

I saw her when I turned around to watch the water shout down at the earth. She and another girl, both carrying tennis rackets, were standing on the other side of 111th Street, waiting for a pause in the traffic. When it came, her friend hurried across first, running under the custard-stand eave a few feet away from where I stood. But Una, once she had crossed the street, became momentarily blinded by the rain. As she reached the custard stand, she ran directly into me.

She apologized for bumping into me as her fingers brushed the wet hair back from her face, exposing a smile that wrapped its warmth around me. I said something like, "Yeah, it sure is raining out there." I've always had this incredible ability to come up with a witty remark at just the right time.

I offered to buy her a custard. She accepted. What flavor? Chocolate? Ah, already, we had so much in common. Somewhere during that custard, I decided that when I became president, I was going to make that custard stand, and every other ounce of ground that Una ever walked on, a national monument.

It wasn't a case of "love at first sight." I must have known Una at least five minutes before I was wild about her. I'm not going to explain why I felt that way. It can't be done. Being "wild" about someone is not a "why" thing.

Finishing her custard, Una introduced me to her friend. I then introduced Paul Zeppl to both of them. The usual "nice to meet you" crap. Una said that she and her friend had to get going. I asked her for her phone number, saying that I'd like to call her sometime. That would be nice,

Una replied. By then the rain had diminished to a drizzle. Una and her friend began walking home.

Fifty feet away from the custard stand was a phone booth. That night its glass skin was speckled with raindrops. I told Paul Zeppl that he'd have to go home by himself. Waiting forty minutes to make sure she was home. Dialing her number. By the time our conversation ended, the phone booth once again had a clear complexion.

Una lived six blocks away from me in a small pink frame bungalow that snuggled between two huge floppy trees resting on the front lawn. During the summer, after dinner, I'd go over to her house and we'd take long walks through the neighborhood. Afterward we'd return to Una's house and sit on her front porch and talk until exactly five minutes before I had to be home at 10:30. At 10:25 I'd say goodnight to Una and then sprint the six blocks to my house, arriving within seconds of 10:30. If Una had lived a few more blocks away, I might have gone to college on a track scholarship.

After I learned to drive, whenever I entered the neighborhood to return to my house, I always drove by Una's first. During the times that we weren't seeing each other I still went by her house, even if I had to drive blocks out of my way to do it.

Una was, in my opinion, absolutely scrumptious. One of the unique things about her was that my opinion, and no one else's, was all that mattered to me. Although some guys saw Una as simply an attractive girl with a nice personality, I looked upon her more realistically as living proof of the brilliant work that God could do when He really set His mind to it.

Every time Una came to the door, she looked more

beautiful than she had the time before. As I got older I started taking Una on real dates, something more than a Little League game or the local miniature golf course. After I brought her home and said goodnight to her on the front porch, she would step inside and quietly ease the front door shut. I'd walk down the steps, pause for a few seconds, and then return to her door and knock lightly, just to see her face again. And Una, knowing me well, would be listening for my footsteps.

She always wore a certain kind of perfume. I don't know what it was. Una was the only one I knew who wore it. I would have liked the fragrance anyway. But since it became synonymous with Una's presence, during the early minutes of being with her my nostrils would become completely enchanted on one leisurely, lung-filled inhale.

A few years ago I was riding a New York subway. My hand was holding tightly onto the overhead strap when my nostrils detected, through that slime of smells that passes for air down there, the fragrance of Una. Looking around I discovered that the source of the perfume was an old lady sitting in front of me. Strange, Una's fragrance without Una. I didn't realize I was staring at the old lady until she looked up at me, smiled, and said, "Weirdo."

Not every guy in the world wanted Una, only about half of them. Most were of the Pat Boone variety: pure, wholesome, homogenized, and taller than me. Whenever I learned the first name of one of them ("Who was that guy I saw you with last week?" "Oh, that was Bob. . . .") I'd immediately hate every guy in the world with that first name. At no time did my relationship with Una contain even a shadow of rationality.

Una and I never dated for more than a few months at a time. We didn't get along very well. We'd see each other for a few months, have an argument, and then break off our relationship. Months later we'd start the whole thing over again. Perhaps both of us had seen too many Doris Day movies and felt compelled to constantly reenact the old "boy meets girl, boy loses girl, boy gets girl" jazz. Possibly my feelings grew so intense that it made communications between us difficult. Maybe I was a jerk.

When I was a kid, life was a series of valleys and peaks. The valleys held such things as rainy Monday mornings, nothing to do, having to dry the dishes during a good television show, and unfinished homework. Peaks came in the forms of Friday afternoon feelings, visiting my grandfather, and eating in restaurants.

Growing older, much older, the valleys have gradually risen and the peaks have slowly dwindled as my existence has leveled out into one long straightaway. Comfortable but dull. Occasionally, looking back, I can see that the highest peaks and the lowest valleys belong to Una.

9

AMONG OTHERS, SMOOTH EDDIE

Most of the teachers at Bremmer High School were made in a cardboard factory and shipped in from Muncie, Indiana. They showed up every day, maintained classroom control, took roll call, assigned and collected homework, asked and answered questions, read and had us read the textbook, held parent-teacher conferences, and handed out grades. They trained us well but rarely did any teaching. They could have stood in front of a mirror and not have seen a thing. There were a few members of the faculty, however, who definitely cast reflections.

At Bremmer old religious brothers, like old soldiers, never died but instead just faded away. The fading process began when a brother became too ancient to teach a full schedule of classes and was assigned to Room 238 to teach three sections of typing each day. When the last few letters of the alphabet began getting hazy, the aging brother was made chief librarian. When he got too decrepit to put any power behind the date-due stamp, he was made assistant vice-principal of the school. The sole responsibility of that position was to answer the phone in the office when the secretaries were on a break or out to lunch. When his mind finally skidded down to the level where he could no longer hear the phone ringing, or didn't care if it did, he was sent to the main monastery in upper New York state, which was the order's mausoleum for the living.

In sophomore year I took typing from Brother Sens who had been, for years, the oldest teacher at Bremmer High School. Short and wrinkled, he looked more like a toy accordion than he did a member of a religious order. The skin on his face was a naked pink, as if it had just been slapped by the breath of a cold winter day. His face was always dressed in a subtle tension that could have passed for either a smile or a sneer. You could never be quite sure which one it was. But it was the same facial expression that was worn by the guys who wore black leather jackets and hung around the drugstore up on the corner.

For over forty years the St. Bremmer religious order had tolerated Brother Sens' classroom presence in a number of their high schools across the country. At every school the students found Brother Sens to be highly amusing but slightly strange, while the administration thought that he was extremely strange and not at all amusing. Among Catholic religious orders, however, it was not considered very kosher to toss out the sickies once they had taken their final vows.

The problem was that Brother Sens found life basically boring and so spent a good part of it trying to amuse himself. He was a good teacher when he felt like teaching, which wasn't very often. If Brother Sens wasn't in the mood to impart academic information, he would tell his students tales about his brothers and sisters (he was from a family of sixteen) or shoot the bull about the

Brooklyn neighborhood where he had grown up or any other topic that alighted within his head.

During one of Brother Sens' classes, a minor auto accident occurred on the corner outside his classroom window. Brother Sens seized the opportunity and turned it into a learning experience for his students. He told them that if they ever had the misfortune to run over a pedestrian, the first thing they should do is back the car up and run over the guy again. "If you just wound him," said Brother Sens, "he can sue you for a couple of hundred thousand. But if you kill him, it's a flat ten thousand. So if you hear 'bump-ta-bump' under your wheels, throw that damn thing into reverse and go 'bump-ta-bump' again."

Religious brothers, since they had taken the vow of poverty, received no salary. At that price, even Brother Sens was a bargain.

Throughout his forty-year teaching career, many of Brother Sens' fellow religious members thought that he was crazy. While teaching at Bremmer High School he turned sixty-five, and Brother Purity decided that Brother Sens wasn't crazy after all; he was senile. Instead of easing Brother Sens out of the teaching business by first assigning him to the typing room and then the library, Brother Purity immediately dropped him into the preserve jar labeled "assistant vice-principal." Brother Sens reacted predictably, for Brother Sens.

Many of the phone calls that came into the school office were from mothers who were calling to explain why their sons were absent from school. Such a phone call was required by school policy. The first mother to talk to Brother Sens explained to him, for twenty minutes, how her son had caught a cold and how he was suffering from a sore throat and a running nose. When the mother paused momentarily to refuel her lungs, Brother Sens commented, "I certainly hope that he lives and that his tuition's paid up in full gobble gobble gobble." A few hours later, when he was called into Brother Purity's office, Brother Sens started off the conversation by reciting the alphabet. Brother Purity got the message. The next day Brother Sens was the new typing teacher.

Brother Sens believed that to be a good typist you had to develop total concentration. So whenever he gave us an exercise to do, he would attempt to "unconcentrate" us. During the first weeks of class, when we tried to type out an exercise from the textbook, Brother Sens would bounce a volleyball off the back wall of the room. If he caught anybody looking up, he would walk over to the offender and punch him in the head.

Since Brother Sens was old, and a little guy besides, he couldn't punch very hard. But the student being attacked, in order not to offend him, would react like he had been slugged by a sledgehammer. You could tell that Brother Sens wasn't fooled but he went along with the routine anyway.

After a couple of weeks everyone learned to ignore the volley ball being bounced off the back wall; so Brother Sens changed tactics. He began bamming books down on his desk. Those who looked up got punched in the head. But within a few days we also became immune to that distraction.

It was then we discovered that Brother Sens was an accomplished magician. He would place a number of items on his desk, such as a pencil, an eraser, and a book, and by simply passing his hand over the desk would make them disappear. If any student looked up from his typing exercise to watch, he would promptly be rewarded with the usual punch on the head.

After a few months Brother Sens was finding it almost impossible to invade our concentration. One afternoon during a timed-speed exercise, he clutched his throat and began gasping for breath. The student who ran to his aid got punched in the head.

By spring there was no way that Brother Sens could interrupt any of us during a typing exercise. Now, while we typed an exercise, he would wander around the front of the room with a pained expression on his face as if he were waiting for someone to clear out of the bathroom.

The only kid in our class who did not become an excellent typist was Jarvis Honbol, and Brother Sens could hardly be held responsible for him. Although Jarvis was of normal height, he had size-fifteen hands. When he placed both of them on the desk you couldn't even see the typewriter. A Jarvis Honbol finger had to hit at least three keys at a time.

On the last day of class Brother Sens went around the room and punched every kid in the head so that no one could claim he played favorites.

I don't know whether Brother Sens is still alive today. I doubt it. He'd be extremely old. But when he did decide to die, I'm sure he was in the prime of life.

The salary of a lay faculty member at Bremmer High School was fairly low, approximately eight dollars a year and all the holy cards he could eat. The average lay teacher was young, somewhere in his twenties, was still going to school for an advanced degree, and, as soon as he got it, would quit teaching at Bremmer. With such a brisk turnover in help, a few like Mr. Douglas Blair were able to slip through the scrutiny of Brother Purity's personal interview.

Today there are many facts of the animal world that still remain beyond the comprehension of our best scientists. No one can explain, for instance, how salmon swim thousands of miles back to their original spawning grounds, why ants have such highly structured social system, or what Elizabeth Taylor saw in Eddie Fisher. Nor is there a mind among men that can explain how a group of students instinctively sense that a teacher, who has just stood before them for the first time, has no idea of what he is doing.

I had Mr. Blair for World History in junior year. He appeared to be in his early forties, much older than most of the other lay teachers. He had the walk and shape of a middle-aged woman. But when he talked his voice seemed to whine out across his lips. So, although Mr. Blair was old enough to have been my father, he looked like my mother and talked like my little sister.

On that first day of class Mr. Blair did so many things wrong that he might as well have written on the board, "I'm a pushover; take advantage of me." He had hardly stepped into the classroom when he made the most fundamental mistake a teacher can make. He smiled. Educational etiquette demands that a teacher never smile until Christmas at the earliest, unless he is in the process of beating up on someone or is handing a student an expulsion notice.

Mr. Blair followed up that mistake with an even bigger one. He revealed facts about his personal life. Mr. Blair told us that he had a wife and three children. A teacher who knows what he's doing gives his students the impression that the moment he finishes his teaching day, he steps onto another planet and doesn't come back to earth again until his next class. The reason for such secrecy is obvious. Students are natural mockers. The more they know about a teacher, the more they can mock him.

Ten minutes after he began teaching, a few guys started goofing off in the back of the room. Mr. Blair looked up from his notes and said, "Now, boys. . . ." I don't remember what he said after that. It didn't matter. Mr. Blair had gone down for the third time. "Now, boys" were the words of a man who thought that he was dealing with a group of rational human beings rather than with high school juniors. For the rest of Mr. Blair's brief teaching career at Bremmer High School, he played straight man to forty different comedians an hour.

"Order, boys, order."

"A Coke and fries."

"Now, boys, I don't want to see any fooling around."

"Mr. Blair, would you mind turning around?"

"Who knows what President Roosevelt's biggest problem was?"

"Mrs. Roosevelt."

Cutting classes at Bremmer was serious business. If you got caught it meant an automatic suspension. Not many students, therefore, attempted it, except those in Mr. Blair's class.

Mr. Blair never looked up from the lectern as he called out each student's name from the attendance sheets. Jack Schroeder was in Mr. Blair's class with me. Jack had been born with an unusual talent. He was an expert at throwing his voice. He had also come into the world with a strange sense of humor. You'd be walking

153

down the hall with Jack and you'd suddenly become aware of people staring at your crotch because voices were coming from it.

Every afternoon four or five guys would cut Mr. Blair's class and Jack Schroeder, tossing his voice in various directions, would answer roll call for them. One day, when I was sitting next to Jack during homeroom period, he told me about the terrific dream he had had the previous night about Mr. Blair's class. Jack had dreamt that he had answered roll call for the entire class and he wasn't even there himself.

After enduring three months of our continuous classroom carousing, Mr Blair finally figured out a way to get even with us. He quit.

On a Monday afternoon we filed into Room 214, flopped down into our seats, and waited for the body to arrive that had been hired to replace Mr. Blair. Just as the bell rang for the beginning of class, a short muscular man built like a thumb walked through the door. His body was accompanied by a pencil stuck behind an ear, an unzipped winter jacket, a checkered sport shirt unbuttoned at the top, gray work pants, white socks, and metal-tipped work shoes. Even though his hands were empty, I automatically wondered what had happened to the package he was supposed to be delivering.

He stopped in front of the lectern, yanked out a grade book that he had folded in his back pocket, and dropped it onto the face of the lectern. A couple of guys started whispering in the back of the room. The man at the lectern lifted his head as the words stomped out of his mouth. "You two looking to get your asses kicked?" The party was over.

As he took roll call, the sounds from his throat moved at us like thugs. He was the only teacher I ever had who could intimidate a class just by calling out their names.

After finishing the roll call he announced, "I'm Ed Kascher, your new World History teacher. Take some notes." For the rest of the class and the duration of that week, Ed Kascher, without any notes of his own, talked about the history of mankind and why it was important that we learn about it.

When he lectured, his works, stripped of the usual human rhythm, fell out of his mouth like rocks. We had to concentrate on and momentarily remember each of his words so that we could couple them into ideas. But as those rocks continued to fall they gradually began to build, within our minds, a monument to Ed Kascher or, as he soon became known among the students, "Smooth Eddie."

The faculty couldn't stomach Smooth Eddie. He dressed like a slob, used obscene language, ate like an animal, didn't show respect for anyone or anything, and constantly made smart-ass remarks. In other words, he was just like one of the students.

During a lunch hour some of the staff people, including Smooth Eddie and the two women secretaries who worked in the office, were eating lunch in the faculty room. Mr. Kila, the young Social Studies teacher, came in and sat down at the table across from Smooth Eddie. Mr. Kila had been in the seminary until a year before he came to Bremmer High School. He had dropped out a month before he was to be ordained because he felt that he no longer had a vocation. Three months later he married a nursery-school teacher he had met in a supermarket. He enjoyed telling people how he fell in love in

155

front of the frozen-foods section. Mr. Kila had a moral standard that God would have envied. He once told a class that he didn't think ten commandments were enough. During his first week at Bremmer he overheard a student say "damn." Mr. Kila went to Brother Purity and asked that the student be expelled and that charges be placed against him.

Mr. Kila's personality was composed of one part happy and one part concerned. He was always one or the other. That day in the faculty room, his "concern" was temporarily submerging his standard tin smile.

"Last night I was making up my lesson plans for next week," Mr. Kila announced to no one in particular, "and I realized that the next chapter we're going to be covering is on marriage and the family. After looking through the textbook, and all the reference books I have at home, would you believe I couldn't find a definition of the perfect marriage. I don't know what to do. What am I going to tell the boys next week?"

"Don't worry, Kila," said Smooth Eddie, "I got the definition of a perfect marriage for you."

"Gee, do you? That's great, Ed. Not only can I use it with my students, but it might also help me in my relationship with Margaret."

Already a few of the faculty who knew Smooth Eddie's ways were crouching low in anticipation of the flak that was about to fly. The two secretaries, both caught in midbite, dropped their sandwiches back onto the wax paper. Their hands scurried for lunch bags and purses. But the fingers couldn't outrace Mr. Kila's enthusiasm.

Mr. Kila took a notebook pad and a pen out of his shirt pocket. "Go ahead, Ed," said Mr. Kila who was now ready to write down the words, "give me that definition of a perfect marriage."

So Smooth Eddie did. Mr. Kila took such a gasp that he almost created a vacuum inside the faculty room. From that day on, the two secretaries never again ate lunch in the faculty room. Mr. Kila was so grossed out that he simply never ate again.

After spending the first two weeks lecturing at us, Smooth Eddie went around the room one afternoon pointing to each student and then calling out the name of a country. "Jaski, Portugal; O'Connor, Finland; Algone, Ethiopia. . . ." We were then told to study, for the next few weeks, the history of the particular country that we had been assigned. After that, said Smooth Eddie, our class, representing the forty major countries of the world, would get the chance to rewrite history from the year 1900. Each of us, knowing the social, economic, political, and geographical abilities of our assigned countries, would interact with the other nations of the room and try to improve our country's conditions. All of us would receive grades in a number of areas such as "Economic Improvement" and "Political Stability."

We didn't do so well. Our room of nations had four world wars and two international depressions lasting twenty years apiece. The only major incident occurred in the hallway after class. France, after a particularly trying day on the battlefield, punched Italy into a locker. France got an "A" in warfare and an "F" in diplomacy.

Smooth Eddie also told us his foolproof system for ending all wars. He called it the "Great Goldfish Bowl Antiwar System." International law would demand that every country have a huge goldfish bowl. If a nation went to war, the names of all its adult citizens, including its politicians, would be tossed into it. When one of that country's soldiers was killed on the battlefield, a citizen's name would be drawn out of the goldfish bowl and he would be killed, too. If a soldier was blinded in combat then a citizen would be chosen by lottery and blinded. With the "Goldfish Bowl Antiwar System" everyone, from the President on down, would be taking the same chances as the guy who was doing the actual fighting. Such a system, said Smooth Eddie, would quickly end all wars. Smooth Eddie said that he got the idea for the system from watching a television quiz program that told home viewers they could participate in the game by mailing in a postcard.

Smooth Eddie even knew when not to teach. Midway through one of his classes, a bland sky suddenly became congested with bands of roving, big-boned storm clouds. The sun backed off and the earth grew gray and cowered below as the storm clouds began rumbling into one another. Winds, whipped up by the confrontations, huffed against the school's windowpanes as they tried to escape from the upcoming holocaust.

A few were feigning interest in what Smooth Eddie was saying, but most of us had openly surrendered to the fascination of the developing storm. Smooth Eddie stopped talking, walked over to a window, and along with the rest of us began observing the mounting turbulence. Only wind and the muffled threats of the storm clouds continued to violate the sanctity of the observance.

One small cloud squeezed off a flash of lightning. A chain reaction of violence erupted across the sky. Lightning, thunder, hail, and rain repeatedly whammoed the world around us. With minds as clear as the sky was cluttered, we silently sat mesmerized by the brutality of the moment. Within a few minutes it was over. Ripples of blue sky pushed the war-worn clouds apart as slivers of sunlight slipped through their souls. The wind lay exhausted and birds once again found the courage to sing.

That was Smooth Eddie. You could have a more meaningful class with him just standing by the window than you could get from other teachers knocking their brains out.

Toward the end of the semester, Smooth Eddie spent five or six class periods talking about how the various minority groups, especially the Blacks, had been mistreated throughout the history of our country. During these lectures Smooth Eddie recited the facts and never once expressed any of his own opinions on the subject matter.

Friday afternoon we were scheduled to write an essay examination on the subject. Thursday was scheduled to be used as a review day. Smooth Eddie was to go over all the material and answer any questions that we might have. Actually most review days turned out to be bull sessions since very few of us bothered to ask questions. But on that review day there was no goofing around. After roll call Smooth Eddie talked about the South Side neighborhood where he had grown up.

"It was an old neighborhood and a poor one, too. But everybody kept up their property. My mother had a garden in the backyard, just behind the porch, where she used to raise vegetables.

"Many of the families were into their second generation there. Mine was. My father was born on the second floor of a two-flat that was just ten doors away from the house where we lived. My mother had grown up three blocks away. I had cousins in the neighborhood, too.

"It was a place where everybody was always walking somewhere. If you didn't have anything else to do, you could just sit on your front porch and talk to friends of yours as they walked by.

"You knew everybody by their first name. I used to love going up to the corner store to talk to Mr. Fazi, this old Italian man who ran it.

"I knew every inch of that neighborhood. What the hell, I spent the first eighteen years of my life living all over it."

Smooth Eddie's voice grew menacing. "Then the niggers started moving in. In less than two years, they turned the neighborhood into a goddamn slum. I drove by my old house once and I could hardly recognize it. When I went down the alley, I could see that my mother's garden was nothing more than a mud pit. About a week later, Mr. Fazi was killed in a stickup."

Smooth Eddie paused a second, began to speak again but then changed his mind. He slipped his hands into his back pockets. "Read your notes till the bell rings." He sat down in his chair, dropped his feet on the desk top and stared at the ceiling.

The following day we took the essay exam. On Monday afternoon we sat before Smooth Eddie as he fingered through our papers. "These goddamn things reek, you know that." Smooth Eddie was pissed. "For a month I give you guys nothing but facts, facts, facts. One day, I give you feelings and you remember those and forget everything else. When I ask you guys questions on a test, I want you to give me answers that are supported by hard facts, not a lot of emotional bullshit. Save your emotions for your broad when you take her to the drive-in. In here your feelings better damn well be based on facts and not the other way around." He walked over to the wastepaper basket and threw in the stack of exams. "There'll be another test on the same material this Friday."

Even at the time I was in class, I thought that Smooth Eddie was a damn good teacher. A few years after high school, I felt he was a great one. Today I realize that he was the only one.

10

DOUBLE-DATING WITH
FELIX LINDOR

In junior year, during a Social Studies class, we were listening to a lecture on male adolescence. "According to the latest research," said Mr. Gorshing, our instructor, "the average male teen-ager in our society has a sexually related thought once every seventeen seconds."

Everyone in the class was visibly shocked by Mr. Gorshing's statement, even Felix Lindor, who was sitting three seats over from me. That's impossible, I thought to myself. Whoever did that research doesn't know what he's talking about.

Just then the bell in the hall began braying. We all scooped up our books from the ramps beneath our seats and began shuffling toward the door. Felix was in front of me. "One sexual thought every seventeen seconds," I said to Felix. "Man, that's hard to believe."

"It sure is," he replied. "What would you do with the other sixteen seconds?"

Felix the Filth Fiend Lindor started taking an interest in the opposite sex the moment he realized which one he was opposite. Before he was old enough to attend school himself, he was already hanging around playgrounds with his pockets full of candy. In grammer school, during a civics class, the nun once asked Felix what would be the first legislative act he'd pass if he were a congressman. Felix said he'd outlaw slacks.

At some point in a male's life he realizes that certain parts of a female's anatomy have become more appealing to him than others. Some men come to consider themselves "leg" men and choose their women accordingly, while others label themselves "breast" or "ass" men and seek out girls with the appropriate fixtures. Not Felix Lindor. He was an "everything" man. If there was blood running through it, he was interested.

There wasn't a facet of Felix Lindor that wasn't lewd. Even the way he laughed was cruddy. When Felix chuckled you automatically looked around to see whose pants had fallen down.

By the time I was a junior in high school I had, like most guys my age, discovered and cultivated the traditional moves of a young man on the make. At the beginning of the evening when I drove up to a date's home, I would always have the driver's side of the car facing the house. That way, when I walked her back to the car, it would seem natural for me to open the driver's door to let her in. If she wanted to be a "door-hugger," then she was going to have to earn it by dragging her rear end across the entire front seat.

On double dates when I was driving, the other couple were taken home first, even if both of them lived on my block.

I also subscribed to the "Graduated Touching Date System." A "touching date" was one where, in the normal course of events, you were allowed to touch your date—not the most interesting parts of her, perhaps, but at least you got to touch her somewhere.

The most common and impersonal touching date was

one that involved slow dancing. Slow-dance touching was the least intimate form of touching because it was demanded by the situation. You've got to touch to slow dance. The more mandatory the touching is, the less intimate it is.

A more intimate touching date was the amusement park. Take a girl on a ferris wheel or an equally reckless ride and you could get away with putting your arm around her or squeezing her up close to you.

Still higher on the intimacy scale was taking a girl to a show, if you did it right. You could, of course, go to a show and do no touching at all. But if you did do some touching, hand holding, arm around shoulders, or better, then the touching was definitely of a higher quality than the amusement park variety.

At the amusement park you may have done the touching before your date had even realized what was happening. Rather than cause a commotion, she might have chosen to just go along with it. She could also rationalize in her mind that the reason you were hanging all over her was that you were trying to protect her from the ravages of the ferris wheel. But touching at the show was different. It was the silence of the situation. The instant you did something, she knew it. More importantly, she knew that you knew she knew it.

The top touching date was the drive-in. When you asked a girl to go to the drive-in, it was just another way of asking her if you could touch her. A successful night at the drive-in was when all you could remember of the movie was the sound track.

If you wanted to take the average Catholic girl to a drive-in, you had to spend weeks and months creeping up her ladder of dating intimacy until you got high enough to grab everything you wanted. Only after a substantial investment of time and money did you often discover that you were dating a girl with a footstool morality.

Some Catholic girls would park and neck and all of that, but only with a guy they considered their "steady." You had to put in your time.

The only possible way you could actually score with the average Catholic girl was if you had been dating her from the moment you were both still warm from the womb. And sometimes not even then.

In today's world of free-flowing flesh all of this may sound absurd, but that's the way it was. There were, of course, a few easy marks among the Catholic girls. The nuns and priests called them "bad girls." Mothers referred to them as "bums" and "tramps." Other girls called them "loose." A few of the boys called them often. But most of us guys avoided such girls. We had been indoctrinated to believe that something that was easy to get wasn't worth getting. Besides, there were many of us who were afraid that if we did have an opportunity to get it, we wouldn't quite know what to do with it.

Like everyone else I knew, I tried to date girls of a higher quality than my looks, social status, or personality could ever have justified. When I wasn't successful on that level I'd reluctantly associate with girls in my own social class. Never, however, did I dare risk dating a girl who was socially beneath me. To do so would have been deliberately running the risk of contracting the fatal dating disease known as the Gavelli Syndrome.

In freshman year Chester Gavelli was the nucleus of the neighborhood social whirl. He was average looking, a fair athlete, and a mediocre student. He was also reasonably proficient in the social skills, such as fast dancing and shooting the bull, and possessed a passable, though certainly, unspectacular, personality. Chester Gavelli was an average guy who, for no reason at all, became the most popular person in the neighborhood. It happens all the time. His only outstanding characteristic was that he always associated exclusively with Grade "A" girls.

Chester Gavelli was, of course, very much aware of the fact that he was a social hotshot. A big part of being a hotshot is knowing it. But one day Chester Gavelli did something that no hotshot should ever do. He wondered why.

The decline was gradual. He began dating a girl who wasn't quite as prime as the other fillets. A couple of months later he started seeing another girl who was a few social notches lower than the previous one. Three weeks after that Chester's quality control went totally berserk when he began dating Diane Basbend, who actually looked like her school I.D. picture.

Realizing that he was out of her league, Diane Basbend did the only thing that any sane person would have done. She dropped Chester Gavelli, thus sending her own social stock skyrocketing while causing Chester's to disintegrate.

Felix Lindor ignored all these social games. He never concerned himself about when he should try to take a girl on a major touching date. He didn't go on any other kind. Felix had even been known to take a girl to a Christmas midnight Mass and, just before the Gospel, try to cash in on her holy spirit.

Nor did Felix worry about the Gavelli Syndrome. Unlike the rest of us, Felix went after girls of all social levels; high class, low class, no class. There was hardly a girl on the South Side of Chicago who didn't know Felix at least by his reputation. All of them, the untouchables, the knockouts, the mousy brown-haired ones and the fatties, knew what he was after but went out with him anyway. Felix Lindor seemed to have a license on lechery.

Felix rarely talked about his exploits. Like all true artists he performed only for the benefit of himself.

Sitting in study hall, next to Felix Lindor. On the table before me was a college sociology textbook that I had borrowed from my older sister. I had planned on looking through it to find an idea for a social studies paper that was due in two weeks. Instead I had turned to the index in the back of the book and had copied down all the pages that were listed under "sex." I didn't usually do that sort of thing, but I always got a little dusty when I sat next to the world's dirtiest mind.

"Hey, Ryan," Felix whispered, "what are you doin' a week from Saturday night?"

"Uhhh, nothing that I can rember. Why?"

"How about doubling with me? I got a date with this new broad, but I can't get the old man's car."

"Gee, I don't know, Felix. I'm not dating anyone in particular right now and. . . ."

"Oh, can't get a girl, uh? Okay, I was just asking. . . ."

"I didn't say that. If it's that important to you, I'll get a date."

"Thanks, Ryan, you're a real pal."

I was a real sucker. Ever since I was a kid, I could never resist the compulsion to walk through a mud puddle rather than around it.

The following day I was sitting on my front steps with

Timmy Heidi when I mentioned to him that I was doubling with Felix.

"Good luck," said Heidi.

"Why?"

"I doubled once with him last year. He's an embarrassing guy to be around."

"What do you mean?"

"He just makes you feel very uncomfortable. All night I felt like I was standing up to my shoulders in a swamp."

I asked out Barbara Reigel. We had gone through grammar school together. I didn't know her very well, though, because she lived on the other side of the neighborhood. Barbara had been dating the same guy since she had been in high school. They were even beginning to look like one another. His name was Nelson and he went to a military high school somewhere in Kansas. She did date other people occasionally, including myself, but always began such dates by informing the individual that she and Nelson had an "understanding" that they would date "other people." What better way to spend an evening than wallowing in the footsteps of a legend. But she was attractive and pleasant enough to be with. I just needed a date for that night, not a three-year, no-cut contract.

Felix was taking out Cynthia Scluzz, the most notorious "give-it-away" girl in the neighborhood. With Felix and her, it was strictly a case of sleazy meets easy. Cynthia wasn't too bright. The most intelligent sounds that came through her mouth were the burps from her Pepsis.

Cynthia's family had just moved four blocks, from 109th and Spaulding to Felix's street. Her father wanted to be closer to his job. He worked at one of the neighborhood's gas stations. When Felix and I picked her up, I kidded her about living on the same block as Felix.

"You know, Cynthia, living on the same street is like being related."

"Really?" she asked.

"Well, it's almost like being related."

"Will you cut the crap," said Felix. "She'll believe anything you tell her."

"That's not true," said Cynthia. She looked over at me. "Is it really almost like being related?"

After picking up Barbara, the four of us went to the show to see a double feature of westerns. Felix and Cynthia deliberately sat behind Barbara and me instead of in the same row. Five seconds into the show, Barbara and I could feel moans drifting in from behind us.

"What's that sound I hear?" she asked.

"Pardon me?" I had heard her. I was just stalling for a little extra time to think up something to say.

"I said, what's that sound?"

"You mean the moaning?"

"Yes, that's right."

"That's Felix. He always moans when he goes to the show."

"He does?"

"Yeah. It's the popcorn. The kernels get caught in his throat; so he moans to try and shake them loose."

"Oh, I see. Does Cynthia eat popcorn, too?"

At the intermission the two girls went running off to the washroom, naturally. They're all like that. Every few minutes it's off to the washroom. They must have divining rods built inside of them.

Felix leaned over Barbara's vacated seat. "Hey, Ryan,

what do you wanna do after this?"

"Get something to eat, I suppose."

"Let's go park somewhere."

"I can't do that. I don't know Barbara that well."

"You will after we've parked a while."

"Naw, I wouldn't feel comfortable sitting in the front seat with Barbara while you were taking Cynthia apart in the back seat."

"Look, Ryan, I don't want to offend your goddamn moral standards; so why don't you find a nice secluded place to park and then you and Barbara can take a walk. A real long walk."

"Hey, that's a good idea. But how long do you want us to walk?"

"Till you fall over on your asses."

"You know, Felix, you're. . . ." The girls were coming back from the washroom.

A few hours later we were driving toward Laverall Park, one of Chicago's biggest, which lounged along the edge of Lake Michigan. Huge hunks of rocks cushioned the park from the lake's methodic rumblings. The rocks were piled just below the parking lot whose blackness was punctured by prongs of red parking lights. I started pulling into the lot.

"Not here," Felix protested as he leaned forward from the back seat and slapped a hand on my shoulder. "There's too many people and the cops drive through every three seconds."

"Felix, I know this is a big park but, believe me, there's no part of it that's secluded. I've been here before, you know." I had been, too. Both previous visits, however, had been during the day. I had no idea whether or not there were any secluded sections of the park. I just didn't want to spend the remaining hours of the evening driving around trying to find out.

"Yeah, well take a little drive through the park anyway," said Felix. "Maybe we'll get lucky."

"Okay, Felix," I said stiffly, "but if we don't get lucky real fast, we're coming back here."

"Yeah, yeah."

I began cruising the car along the winding road that rippled through the park. Barbara was getting apprehensive about the entire situation.

"Don't worry," I said to her quietly, "Felix and Cynthia just want to be alone for a while. You and I can take a little walk."

"I'm not worried." She flashed a dollar smile where a dime would have done just as well; so I knew she was lying.

"Pull over here, Ryan." Felix was pounding his hand on my shoulder again.

"Where? Over where? I don't see anything."

"Right there. That dirt road. Turn down there."

"Yeah, I see it now." It seemed strange. All the other roads in the park were paved. "Wait a second, Felix. What if it's a dead end? I'll never be able to back out of there."

"Go in a little way and pull over to the side of the road. That's all."

"Okay." I turned and drove about a hundred yards. But by then the trees were so close to the edge that there was no place to pull off the road. I wasn't too concerned about parking in the middle of the road, though. I suspected that it led to a storage shed that was used by the park's maintenance crew only during the day. I turned off the engine, opened my door, and motioned for Barbara to get out from my side of the car.

"I think that Barbara and I are going to take a walk." The words came out as if they were packed in Styrofoam. Even Barbara looked slightly annoyed at my pretense.

"You do that," Felix mumbled as he turned toward Cynthia, who was already beginning to moan.

I wasn't at all anxious to take the walk with Barbara. I had only dated her three or four times before and those dates had been scattered over a couple of years. We didn't have any trouble finding things to talk about in the car or wherever we went on the date. But a "walking in the park at night" dialogue was something else again. Such moments demanded a much higher caliber of conversation. One that I didn't think Barbara and I were capable of reaching. But we were.

Barbara did most of the talking. She told me about Nelson and why she was so crazy about him. Maybe I should have been insulted. Here I was, her date for the evening and she was talking about some other guy. But as I've already mentioned, her relationship with Nelson was well known. She and I both knew why we were out with each other that night. It beat staying home. As we strolled along the lake's edge, she told me that if her feelings for Nelson didn't change, she would work for a few years after graduating from high school while Nelson went to college. Then they'd get married and start a family after his junior year. She seemed quite pleased with the possibility of spending most of her life loving one man and the children they'd create.

I thought to myself that even if the new year did bring fresh plans, Barbara wouldn't draw her enthusiasm for

173

them by stomping on the old dreams she had previously sheltered. Barbara didn't seem like the kind of person who would turn on herself.

The night wind, which had been bouncing gingerly around the park, was beginning to betray its belligerence. "I'm getting cold," Barbara said. "Why don't we go back to the car?"

"Sure."

"Where the hell have you been?" Felix bellowed as I opened the car door.

"We just took a walk, Felix," I said as I glanced at my watch. We had been gone over an hour. Still, Felix was hardly the guy who I thought would get upset because I had left him alone with a girl too long. "What are you mad about?"

"Nothing," snapped Felix. "Let's get going."

As I adjusted the rearview mirror, I tilted it slightly so that I could see Cynthia. She really looked upset.

Barbara was still cold. She sat with her knees high and her arms folded, the elbows cupped in her hands. I started the engine. "I'm gonna run the car for a few seconds to get some heat in here." No one replied. That was when I heard it, a quiet rumble.

Barbara started to say something. "Wait," I interrupted her as I turned off the engine. "Do you hear anything?"

"Faintly," she replied. "What is it?"

"I don't know, but it sounds very familiar. I just can't place it."

"Yes, it does sound familiar," Barbara said.

"I don't hear nothin'." said Felix.

"Neither do I," agreed Cynthia.

The rumbling was growing louder. I turned toward the back seat. "Now can you two hear it?"

174

"Yeah," they both replied together.

I turned back again toward the steering wheel. The rumbling sounded like it was coming right at us. I pulled on the headlights.

"I remember where I heard it," said Barbara. "At the show tonight."

But it was too late. On the dirt road, which was now fat with headlight glare, we saw at least a dozen horses and their riders pounding toward us. We were parked on a bridle path. One of the horses was running well ahead of the others. As the car lights popped on, the eyes of both the horse and rider swelled into saucers at the sudden appearance of my car. The rider yanked back on the reins. But the horse had just begun to back-pedal when it slammed into the hood of the car. Barbara and I ducked down as one of the horse's hoofs shattered the windshield.

Sitting in the police station with Felix Lindor, waiting for the desk sergent to fill out the forms. A short policeman, who had apparently had to stand on a stack of dollar bills to pass the department's height requirement, walked over to us with a slip of paper in his hands.

"Are you the two guys who were involved in that horse accident at Laverall Park?"

"Yes officer," I said.

"Well, here's the address of the gas station where your car was towed." He thrust the white slip of paper at me.

"Thank you, officer."

"Are your parents coming to pick you up?"

"Yes, sir, they are."

"What about the two girls that were with you?"

"Their parents picked them up at the park, sir."

The policeman turned to walk away.

"Uh, officer, what happened to the horse?" I asked.

Up to that point, the little cop's tone of voice had been official but somewhat friendly. Now, as he looked back and spoke at us, his words dripped with distaste. "It had to be destroyed." He obviously felt that his fellow officers had chosen the wrong one to shoot through the head.

The night could have been worse, I thought to myself. No one got hurt, except the horse. The car wasn't too badly damaged and I didn't get any tickets since the police had decided that the park district should have more clearly marked the bridle path as such. My father would certainly have a few words to say, but that was a small price to pay for allowing a horse to come through my windshield. My thoughts were easing me into a good mood. Good moods make me want to talk.

"Say, Felix, how did you and Cynthia get along tonight?"

"All right."

"All right? Just all right? What was the problem?"

Felix began punching his right hand into his left.

"She'd only go so far, thanks to you, Ryan."

"What do you mean?"

"She said we couldn't really mess around, if you know what I mean, because it would be incest."

"Incest?"

"Yeah, incest. Because of that bullshit you told her about how living on the same block is like being related."

"I told her it was *almost* like being related."

"Yeah, I know. That's what I told her you said. And she told me that if we really messed around, that would be almost like incest, which was too close for her. I told you that broad was too goddamn dumb to kid around with." Felix continued to punch one hand into the other.

I decided to try the impossible—get Felix's mind off sex and how I had just caused him to lose out on some of it. "You know, Felix, that Barbara is quite a girl. I mean, I always knew she was pretty and a nice person to talk to, but until tonight I never realized how neat she really was." I waited for Felix to ask me how I had made such a discovery, but he didn't. He just kept punching his fist into his hand.

"I tell you, Felix," I continued apprehensively, "that Barbara's got a lot of class. They don't make girls like that anymore."

Felix finally stopped punching. "Did you?"

11

RETREAT RETREAT

Although I can't remember it, I'm sure it happened shortly after I was born. Perhaps it occurred the first time I knocked over my cup of milk. Or maybe it was when I tried to pull my sister's nose off. Someone much bigger than me said, "Don't do that, it's not nice. Now aren't you sorry?" Those were the first words to water that seed of solid guilt, buried deep within my cranium, which would shortly grow into a full-size Catholic conscience.

What started as a drizzle quickly swelled to a torrent. "No, don't touch that." "No, you can't eat now." "No, you can't go outside." "No, it's too early." "No No No No No." Presumably, those who rained around me hoped that my conscience would mushroom to such a size that it would eventually snuff out my brain.

The biggest cloudburst was my religion. Going through eight years of Catholic grammar school and Sunday morning sermons was like sitting for all those years in the courtroom of a hanging judge. *Guilty! Guilty! Guilty!* Catholicism was always having to say, "I'm sorry."

When the words of parents, the nuns, priests, and any other adult weren't hailing down on us kids in the neighborhood, we'd rain on each other. One summer day when I was nine years old, Lanner and I were walking down the street when we saw a group of kids, including Cookie Vlitsew, sitting on her front porch. In the middle of the group was an eleven-year-old known as the Cut-Rate Liquor Girl. Her mother ran the Cut-Rate Liquor Store up on 111th Street. The girl had lived in the neighborhood only for six months. For some reason nobody seemed to be able to remember her real name. She and her mother moved out of the neighborhood a few months later with everyone still referring to her as the Cut-Rate Liquor Girl.

Oddly enough the Cut Rate Liquor Girl was built just the way a girl with such a name should have been. She had a shot-glass head and a six-pack body.

As Lanner and I walked up to the porch, I noticed an ant colony between one of the cracks in the sidewalk. Normally I'm a rather tame person and I don't go out of my way to inflict pain on anyone, mainly because I'm not too crazy about it myself. But that day, without even thinking about it, I stepped on the ant colony. I guess we all like to play God occasionally.

By the way, the Cut-Rate Liquor Girl was not one of your great humanitarians. What I had just done to the ants, she had done to kids in the neighborhood.

The Cut-Rate Liquor Girl was horrified. "What did you do that for?"

"I don't know. I just did it," I said. Everyone else on the porch stopped talking to listen.

"You think you're going to get away with something like that?"

"What are you talking about?"

"You think God's going to let you get away with it?"

"I don't think God worries too much about ants."

"God worries about everything that lives."

"Well, yeah, maybe. But I don't think He spends a lot of His time on ants."

"What if God is an ant?"

"You're crazy."

"Did anyone ever tell you that He wasn't?"

"No. But nobody ever told me that He was."

"So there. I might be right. He came down here once as a human being. Why not as an ant?"

"Yeah, you might be right. No, no, I don't think so."

"Well, if I am, God help you."

"God help me? If He's an ant, He's not gonna help me."

"You're right. You're outta luck."

For the rest of the summer I felt guilty about stepping on that anthill, and I had more than one nightmare where I heard God saying to me just after I died. "So you're the clown who squashed my son."

Compared to my younger years, the religion classes at Bremmer High School were a drought. Every member of the faculty who was a religious brother had to teach one section of Religion a day. During the other four periods the brother would teach whatever his subject was, English, History, Science. Since Religion wasn't any faculty member's "subject," very few of the brothers spent any time preparing for their religion classes.

My religion teacher in freshmen years was Brother Sash, who had us read the textbook during the first half of class. In the second half of class he would ask us questions on what we had read. Occasionally Brother Sash would skip all of this and lecture to us on the evils of sex.

He told us that our sex drive was like a tank of gas in a car. "Your tanks may be full to the brim now, boys, but if you're sexually overactive at this age, by the time you reach your thirties you may just run out of gas. You'll be impotent."

Danny Budswell, a Jolly Numbers boy, thought that was a good deal until someone explained to him that Brother Sash wasn't mispronouncing the word "important."

Brother Sash's favorite topic was "self-abuse." The biggest danger of this practice, he said, was that if you did it often enough you would go blind. We knew that wasn't true. If it had been, half the population of the school would have had seeing-eye dogs.

I had Brother Sofeck, the Biology teacher, for Religion in sophomore year. Everyone in that class spent most of of his time trying to keep his breakfast down. Brother Sofeck had a pet rabbit named Lazarus, whose cage was our classroom. Every morning we had to tiptoe through the rabbit droppings to get to our desks.

Brother Sofeck spent most of his Religion classes talking about Biology. On those rare occasions when he did get into Religion, he would resort to terror tactics. One morning, for instance, Brother Sofeck showed us how to avoid mortal sin.

"Now, boys, if you don't want to commit a mortal sin, the kind of sin that sends you straight to hell, all you have to do is carry a pack of matches around with you." As he continued to talk he pulled a pack of matches out of his pocket, yanked a match loose from the binding, and lit it. "If you feel like committing a mortal sin, just light a match and stick your finger in it. . . ." He held the flaming match in front of his eyes. ". . . because that would be just a slight taste of what hell is like. Go ahead. The next time you want to commit a mortal sin, light a match and stick your finger in it. If you like it, if it feels good on your finger, go ahead and commit that mortal sin. Commit all the mortal sins you want. You'll just love it in hell. There, your entire body is engulfed in flames for all eternity."

Brother Sofeck was the first one to so graphically demonstrate to me that tactics of the Mafia and the Catholic Church were so alike: Step out of line with either one and you'd get burned.

He also told us about eternity. "How long is eternity, boys? How long? I'll tell you how long. Imagine that there is a solid steel ball the size of the sun. Not the earth but the sun. The sun, as you know, is one million, three hundred thousand times larger than the earth. Now every thousand years a bird flies up to this massive steel ball and flicks its wing against it. When that bird wears that steel ball into nothingness, eternity is just beginning."

After class, Timmy Heidi gave me a better definition of eternity: listening to Brother Sofeck talk about it.

My Religion teacher in junior year was Brother Falley. He never mentioned the subject. Every day when we came to class he'd tell us to take out a book to study and he'd be with us in a moment. Then he'd pick up a book from his desk and start reading. The "moment" never arrived.

The only Religion classes we had that year came during the two weeks when Brother Sens, the Typing teacher, substituted for Brother Falley. Brother Falley had walked through a glass door and had nearly cut his head off. At the time, he was reading a book.

One thing that annoyed me about religion classes was that if a class got into a debate with the teacher and managed to logically back him into a corner, he'd get out of that corner with the same old statement. "Well, boys, it is, after all, a matter of faith. You either believe it or you don't." End of argument.

We were discussing, with Brother Sens, the idea of the infallibility of the Pope; that is, the Catholic Church's article of faith that when the Pope speaks on matters of faith and morals he is always right. Sure enough, just as Brother Sens was beginning to lose the argument, he said, "Well, boys, it is an article of faith. Either you believe it or you don't. I can't prove it to you logically. It's not a question of logic." His statement was greeted by a chorus of moans backed up by scatterings of "Come on, brother."

"Granted," retorted Brother Sens, "sometimes it doesn't make sense to believe. But there are other times when it makes even less sense not to believe. Faith is a very strange thing. If you haven't got it, it's tough to get. And if you have got it, it's tough to lose."

We could feel a "Brother Sens" story coming on. When he told a story, everyone automatically gathered around the fireplace.

"I have a younger brother named Oliver," said Brother Sens. "Years ago, when we were both very young, we got up early one Easter Sunday morning and went around our yard, looking for the eggs that the Easter Bunny had hidden. Oliver was walking toward a small bush when, suddenly, a rabbit shot out from behind the bush and bounded away. My little brother couldn't believe it. But when he ran behind the bush there it was, an Easter egg. Oliver is now sixty-four years old.

184

Though all the years he's lived have carried evidence to the contrary, Oliver still isn't quite sure about the Easter Bunny."

Brother Mandeau, my Religion teacher in senior year, was one of the few who, every day, taught Religion to his Religion class. One morning Brother Mandeau advised us about the truly desirable assets of a prospective dating partner. He said that we should look for a girl whom we could respect, one who dressed modestly and liked old people. "If you want to know what a girl is really like," said Brother Mandeau, "notice how she treats the other members of her family. That's where the true personality comes out. Don't be fooled by that plastic personality she shows you on dates."

Although we all knew that what Brother Mandeau said was true, I'm sure only the purest of souls among us ever followed his advice. It didn't seem like a very sane idea to go out with an ugly girl and, every time someone looked at her, jump to her defense by saying, "But you should see how she treats her little brother."

In the month of March, senior-year Religion teachers were required to spend at least one class talking about the facts of life. We wondered how Brother Mandeau, who blushed when he had to mention the Immaculate Conception, was going to achieve such a feat.

Since he was a History teacher, Brother Mandeau's classroom was equipped with numerous pull-down maps that were fastened to the walls above the blackboards. As we walked into his room one morning, we saw that all the maps had been completely pulled down. After prayers Brother Mandeau quickly walked past the maps, not even stopping as he gave each one a sharp tug that sent it scampering back up into its metal cylinder. As each map rolled up, it exposed the sexual information that had been written on the blackboard behind it. Brother Mandeau refused to look at any of us as he repeatedly yelled out, "No questions, no questions."

Although Religion classes at Bremmer provided only a trickle of water to help our consciences grow, we were, each year, subjected to a three-day downpour: our annual retreat.

A retreat is when you spend a number of days immersed in spiritual activities. During a retreat day, you attend Mass and other religious services such as the Stations of the Cross. You listen to sermons, which are often identified in the schedule as "conferences," do spiritual readings in the library, and endure a few meditation sessions, which consist of kneeling in the chapel for thirty minutes at a time.

The purpose of a retreat is to offer the individual a spiritual reprieve from the materialistic world he daily lives in. Although many do not, Catholics are encouraged to go on at least one retreat a year.

Some retreats, which run from Friday through Sunday afternoons and require staying overnight, are offered by various religious orders at their monasteries. Retreats are often held at parishes for those Catholics who can't or don't want to attend a retreat that requires boarding. A priest from a religious order will come to a parish and conduct the retreat during the evening hours of a particular week. Then there are school retreats, such as the ones that were given at Bremmer High School.

Retreats at Bremmer were no big thrill, but they certainly beat the alternative, three days of regular classes. When you came to school on the morning of a retreat day, you didn't have to worry about homework, surprise quizzes, getting jugged, or any of the other billions of bristles that threatened to stick you during an ordinary school day.

A retreat day contained a very exact schedule: 8:00 A.M., Mass; 9:00 A.M., Conference; 10:00 A.M. Meditation; 10:45 A.M., Stations of the Cross.... You would walk into school and the retreat schedule would scoop you up and, like an assembly-line belt, automatically carry you through the day.

School retreats were like Holiday Inns. No matter where or when you found them, they were always the same. Even the stories the priests told at the conferences were the same. Two perennial favorites were the "God, this is Jimmy" story and the "Don't get in an accident with dirty pictures in your wallet" monologue.

I first heard the "God, this is Jimmy" story at a retreat that was given to my seventh-grade class.

"There was once a boy named Jimmy," the priest began. "He was an average child, just like any of you. The only thing that he did, that most of you probably never thought of doing, was that every day on his way to school he would step into his parish church, kneel down for a moment in one of the pews, and simply say, 'God, this is Jimmy.' Then he would go out and spend his day doing the same things that you do. He would attend school, play outside with his friends, and help his mother with work around the house. One day as he was crossing the street in front of the church on his way to giving his daily greeting to God, a car came out of nowhere and ran Jimmy over, killing him instantly. As Jimmy lay in the street, people rushed to his side. And do you know what those people heard coming from the sky as they knelt beside him?"

187

The room was silent. Even our breathing had shied away to a whisper so as not to interfere with the words that the priest was about to drop on us.

"Jimmy heard a voice say, 'Jimmy, this is God.'"

I was impressed. I really was. I planned, the very next morning, to apply its moral to my own life. I would step into church and whisper from the first pew, "God, this is Eddie." It never hurts to be on a first-name basis.

An hour later I was walking home with Timmy Heidi, whose words quickly pulverized my awe for the anecdote.

"That sure was a dumb story that Father Brennan told us this afternoon," Heidi said.

"Why do you say that?" I was hardly about to admit to Heidi that I had been duped.

"Let's just say that I never go in and say hello to God, okay?" said Heidi.

"Okay."

"What happens when I die? As my soul heads toward heaven and I yell out, 'God, this is Heidi,' what's He gonna yell back? Who? Some God. He's just like any other person who's in a position to screw you. You gotta brown nose."

At my junior-year retreat I heard the "God, this is Jimmy" story for the fifth time.

The "dirty pictures in the wallet" monologue was about this kid who also got run over by a car and ended up in the hospital with a skull fracture, two broken arms, and two broken legs. His biggest problem, however, was that when he got run over he had dirty pictures in his wallet. I first heard the story during my freshman-year retreat.

"Oh, the anguish that boy must have experienced,"

groaned the priest, "when his parents walked into that hospital room and he realized that they knew he was carrying around such disgusting pictures in his wallet. Being good parents, they eventually forgave him. But that kind of hurt, boys, a parent carries in his heart forever. Ah, the sorrow that must have filled his mother's mind. What his father must have thought of him. Can you imagine how that boy must have felt?"

We certainly could. It was a very squeamish story. The kind you didn't like to think about. Actually the only person I knew who carried dirty pictures around all the time was Felix Lindor. After he heard the talk, Felix took the dirty pictures out of his wallet and put them in an envelope along with a letter, which he stuck in his back pocket. The letter read: "Dear Charlie, I found these pictures in the science book you lent me. They are disgusting. If I were you, I'd tear them up. Signed: Felix Lindor."

The priest hinted that even if the kid had died, it would still have been a very embarrassing situation. Such a fact could hardly be deleted from the eulogy. "Johnny was a good student, was popular among both his teachers and his fellow classmates, was cheerful, kind, and considerate. He led an exemplary Christian life, except for the fact that when he died he had dirty pictures in his wallet."

The only student who relished retreats was Louie Schlang. Louie was thoroughly enchanted by the sound of his own voice. He loved to ask dumb questions. During regular school days he didn't often get the opportunity to serenade himself because his habit was too well known among the faculty. But our retreats were held by priests from various religious orders who came to Brem-

189

mer for only three days out of the year. For Louie, those retreat days were orgies of idiotic inquiries.

"Father, is it a sin to eat meat on Friday if I'm on a ship out in the ocean and we're crossing the date line, well, the front part of the boat is but I'm on the back part of the boat and I'm about to eat a hot dog, but it's not an all-meat hot dog, it's got a lot of filler. . . ."

"Say, Father, if God is all-powerful, can He create a rock so big that He can't lift it Himself? But then, if He can't lift it, how can He be all-powerful?"

"Is it a sin to miss Mass on Sunday, Father, if when I get up I have a headache, not a big one just a small one, and I feel like I'm gonna throw my guts up, but when I take my temperature, I find I'm normal. . . ."

It would have taken more than a 98.6 body temperature to make Louis Schlang normal.

We were only a few months away from graduation when we went on retreat in senior year. Convinced that many of us were going to walk straight from the graduation stage to the altar, the priests who conducted the retreat spent most of their time talking about marriage.

Father Blenzy, who was in charge of the retreat, gave the first talk. As expected, he spent the opening minutes trying to convince each of us that we probably had a religious vocation but were just refusing to listen to God's calling. That's the way it always went. Whenever priests, religious brothers, or nuns talked to you about what you were going to do with your life, they tried to convince you to do with it what they had done.

"But if you feel that you must get married," Father Blenzy continued, "that you absolutely need the release that marriage provides, then by all means, get married.

"Now there are, as you boys know," (we didn't)

"three purposes of marriage, one primary and two secondary. Let's first talk about the two secondary purposes. The first secondary purpose is companionship. The other secondary purpose is the curbing of concupiscence."

None of us knew what "concupiscence" meant, but since it was preceded by "curbing" we knew it must have something to do with sex.

"The primary purpose of marriage," said Father Blenzy, "is, of course, children. That is why God has given us our sexual powers. In order that we may create, with His assistance, souls that may share with Him forever the joys of Heaven. Looked at in those terms, the marriage act is truly beautiful, truly holy. I knew one Catholic couple who confided to me that when they performed the marriage act, they say the rosary together. Isn't that beautiful?"

At the next conference there was a young married couple who were supposed to talk to us about their married life. They first told us about the things they did that annoyed one another. "You know what George does that bothers me? In the morning, he leaves the cap off the toothpaste." She followed up that remark with a few titters as if she had just told you something that was quite personal but at the same time very funny. A few school-spirit nuts tittered back at her. He said something about how she always wanted to watch hour-long television programs while he preferred half-hour shows.

The married couple then talked about the little things they did for one another. For instance, he'd get her flowers for no reason at all. She'd set up the morning newspaper for him on the breakfast table. That kind of stuff. They also said that they thought the marriage act was the most beautiful way of saying they loved each other

191

and that, even if she wasn't in the mood, she was still willing to perform her marital duties.

I thought their entire act was putrid. Any two people who would stand up in front of a few hundred high school seniors and talk about their married life had to be crazy.

After the married couple finished, they asked if there were any questions. Not even Louie Schlang raised his hand. Who would want to ask two crazies a question?

I looked over at Felix Lindor. He wasn't going to ask it, but as he looked her over I could see the question slithering in his mind. "How often do you say the rosary together?"

During the last day of my senior-year retreat, small group conferences on a variety of topics were held in the classrooms. Tom Lanner, myself, and about twenty other guys were listening to Father Rinsbury tell us about Christ's trial before Pontius Pilate. Besides being a priest, Father Rinsbury was also an attorney. He was explaining to us the historical background and personality of Pontius Pilate, the political and legal options that were open to him, and why he acted as he did. It was all very interesting stuff we had never heard before.

Ernie Kogan, the center on the football team, was sitting in the last row. Ernie liked to sit in the front row but he had arrived late, just as we were all sitting down, so he didn't have any choice.

As Father Rinsbury spoke I could hear Ernie Kogan shuffling his feet under the desk. Whenever Ernie was in a place where he didn't feel comfortable, he started pacing, even if he was sitting down. Gradually the sound of Ernie's shuffling feet subsided.

Toward the end of the presentation Father Rinsbury

became very dramatic. "As I've already told you, Pilate, who was the Roman govenor, didn't care one way or the other about the Jews or this man Christ, who claimed to be their king. He just wanted to keep things quiet. If word got back to Rome that the Jews were raising a fuss, Pilate would be held responsible.

"There was a large crowd of Jews outside Pilate's palace demanding that Christ be crucified for claiming to be their king. But Pilate didn't believe that Christ had done anything to warrant crucifixion. To appease the crowd Pilate had Christ viciously whipped. The guards who inflicted the punishment also placed a crown of thorns on Christ's head. Afterward Pilate presented the brutally beaten Christ before the crowd. Pilate thought they would feel sorry for Christ and want Him released. But they didn't.

"Pilate stood before the crowd and spoke to them. 'I find no reason to condemn this man. I'm going to release Him.' But the crowd yelled back, 'Crucify Him, crucify Him.' 'Crucify Him yourselves,' Pilate replied. But the crowd persisted. 'We haven't the power; you must.' 'What?' said Pilate mockingly, 'crucify your king?' 'We have no king but Caesar,' the crowd replied. 'If you do not do this,' they shouted, 'you will not be a friend of Caesar's. Anyone who claims to be a king isn't a friend of Caesar's.'

"Pilate was getting scared. The Jews were implying that if he didn't have Christ executed, he'd be committing treason against Caesar. Pilate washed his hands before the crowd to show that Christ's death would be their doing and not his. Then Pilate gave the order, 'Crucify this Christ.'"

"The dirty sonofabitch."

It was Ernie Kogan's voice. His words froze Father Rinsbury's face. What a lousy time to try and be funny, I thought, as I, along with the others, spun my head around to stare at Ernie Kogan. It was then we saw that Ernie Kogan wasn't trying to be funny.

Uncomfortable because of all the unwanted attention he was receiving, Ernie began shuffling his feet again. Our heads turned back toward Father Rinsbury to see what he was going to do.

He stared at Ernie. "Thank you," he said, "for your act of faith." Then Father Rinsbury quietly continued.

12

MY CAR

In my neighborhood, few of us lived under the illusion that our birth certificates proved we were alive. It was that pompous piece of paper, the driver's license, that definitely proved one's existence to the world. A birth certificate was only good for proving you were old enough to join the Little League or young enough to get into the show for the "under fourteen" rate. It was the driver's license that was considered "proper identification," got you into taverns and gave you a reason for performing that most adult of functions, buying a car.

My parents were against the idea. They felt that I wanted a car so I could race around, drink and neck in it. They were right, of course, which was why I was so desperate to get one.

In order to earn the money that I needed for the car and the insurance, I was working part-time as a busboy at a nearby restaurant. One of my co-workers was Crazy Freddie LeGrand. Quite a few people are nicknamed "Crazy . . ." whatever-their-name-is because other people think it's a cute nickname or something stupid like that. But that wasn't the case with Crazy Freddie. He really was crazy.

Once some guy in a pickup truck came racing down

Crazy Freddie's street and ran directly into the rear end of Freddie's parked car. Freddie, who was sitting in his front window observing all this, jumped up and ran out his front door holding his neck and screaming, "Whiplash!"

Crazy Freddie had a habit of changing cars about as often as most people change the months on their calendars. What he'd do is buy an old car and attach license plates to the bumpers of the car with large clips. That way the plates could be pulled off the car in a hurry. If Crazy Freddie ran out of gas, was involved in an accident, couldn't get the windshield wipers to work, or was caught in a traffic jam, he would jump out of the car, grab his license plates, and take off.

I was unloading a tray of dirty dishes when Crazy Freddie came up to me. "Hey, man, I hear you're looking around for a car to buy."

"That's right, Freddie," I said. No one ever called Freddie "crazy" to his face. The nickname was too apropos to do something like that.

"I got a car parked out in back that maybe you'd be interested in."

"I don't know, Freddie. I got a lot of work to do here." I was stalling. I just didn't want to get near anything that involved Crazy Freddie.

"Come on," he said, "it'll only take a few minutes."

"How come you wanna sell it, Freddie? I thought you only abandoned cars?"

"This one's too nice to abandon. I'd like to keep it for myself, but I can't. I think the car's trying to kill me."

I didn't ask him what he meant by that. After all, Freddie was crazy.

Now I had wasted the last three days going through

196

used car lots with my father. For the kind of money I
had to spend, we hadn't come close to finding anything
that even faintly resembled a car. Worse yet, seventy-
two hours of my life had needlessy passed carless. I was
getting desperate, so desperate that I decided to go out
to the parking lot with Crazy Freddie.

"This is it," said Freddie as we stopped in front of a
hulk of pale-blue steel that seemed to have four wheels
under it. It looked so much like an army tank, I was
tempted to ask Freddie what he had done with the gun
turret.

"I thought you said you didn't want to abandon this
car, Freddie. It looks abandoned already."

"You're a riot," snapped Crazy Freddie. "Come on, do
you want to buy it or not?"

"Does it run?"

"Sure it runs. Do ya' think I'd sell ya' a car that didn't
run?" Freddie thought about that a second, silently answered his own question, and then repeated his statement. "Yeah, it runs."

"Let me drive it around the block."

"Nothing doing," said Crazy Freddy. "I ain't got that
kind of time. Just drive it around the parking lot."

"Okay, okay," I agreed.

The car started right up, after Freddie did something
with a can opener under the hood. It picked up speed
well and handled smoothly on the turns. Of course since
the parking lot was filled, I could only get the car up to
twelve miles an hour.

"Well, what do ya' think?" asked Freddie as I pulled
the car back into its parking spot.

"It seems all right, Freddie." I tried to get out of the
car but the door wouldn't budge.

197

"Sometimes it sticks a little." Freddie promptly slammed his fist into the door just below its handle. The door popped open. "Did ya' notice that hole in the floor on the passenger's side?" he asked.

"I certainly did."

"It's great for getting rid of garbage and stuff. Do you like to wash cars?"

"Not especially."

"Then you'll love the paint job on this one. It looks the same whether you wash it or not."

"What's that terrible smell in the car?" I asked.

"Oh, you don't have to worry about that," said Freddie. "It's just some ice cream I put in the back seat and forgot about a few months ago. You can hardly see where it melted into the seats. You know anything about cars?"

"Enough," I replied curtly. That was a lie. The first time someone asked me if I knew how to tune an engine, I told him I wasn't musically inclined. My knowledge of cars was strictly of an "into" nature. I knew where to put gas into the tank, water into the radiator, and air into the tires.

I didn't admit that to Crazy Freddie. A thorough comprehension of a car's mechanical makeup was a necessary part of any South Side male's repertoire. To confess to such ignorance would have been like telling someone I didn't have to shave in the morning.

Crazy Freddie spent ten minutes with his head stuck under the hood of the car, pointing to different pieces of metal and rattling on about them. I just nodded and "uh-huhed" at the proper times. He never caught on.

We were walking back toward the restaurant. "Do you wanna buy it or not?" asked Freddie.

"I'll have to call my father," I said, which I did a few minutes later. He asked only one question. "Does it run? Then buy it."

After work as I drove the car home, I discovered that the radio received only one frequency and that carried a religious station, which restricted itself to playing the top forty of gospel music.

The car also didn't have much of a pick-up. When the light turned green at an intersection, a pedestrian stayed even with me for the first twenty feet.

My father was standing on the curb when I pulled up in front of the house. As soon as I stopped the car he pried open the hood, took one fast look, and then slammed it back down.

"You got the key to the trunk?" he asked.

"Sure, dad." It took both of us to pry it open. It was crammed with junk: an old house fan, greasy engine parts, a bicycle wheel, a crumpled newspaper. My father and I almost had to sit on the top of the trunk to get it closed.

"I can't tell if the engine's in front or in back," he said.

"It's in the front, dad."

"Oh." He just stood there staring at my car. "It certainly has a lot of dents in it," he said.

"It's been in a few accidents, dad. None of them serious, of course."

"Of course," he replied spiritlessly as he began walking back toward the house.

"Do you think I've gotten my money's worth, dad?" I shouted after him.

"How far is it from here to the restaurant?"

"About five miles."

"You've already gotten your money's worth."

I looked back at the car. Its sides were lumped and bruised from previous collisions. Its skin was tainted with large gashes of rust. Wisps of smoke drifted from the engine, which was still out of breath from the ride home. The right headlight was badly cracked. Teeth were missing from the grille. A shock absorber had snapped, causing the car to lean heavily to one side. The tires were bald with fatigue.

I went over to the driver's side, punched the door, opened it, and slid onto the seat. I put my foot on the gas pedal and wrapped my fingers into fists around the steering wheel. Yes sir, there was one thing about this car that made up for all its flaws. It was mine.

That night I had a date with Laura, a fine-looking young thing that I happened to be dating at the time. As we came down the steps of her front porch she stared at my car and then said, "Why, that's a very nice car. It really is." Maybe she meant it. Laura wasn't any brighter than I was about such things.

As I held the door open for Laura I said to her in my most solemn voice, "Enter into the kingdom that has been prepared for you for all eternity." She got a big charge out of that. Laura was such an easy girl to please.

Gradually I began saying that every time I opened the car door for her at the beginning of the evening. It became a little ritual we both thoroughly enjoyed.

That night's date was the first of many that my car shared with Laura and me. It messed up almost every one of them. Before I had my own car, I used my father's. Laura and I would usually spend the last part of the evening either parked in some lovers' lane or on one of the side streets near her house. But my own car made such activities impossible.

Parking in a lovers' lane was out because I could never depend on my car starting. If it didn't, I had to ask some other guy who was also parking in the lovers' lane for help. Since he had better things to do, he was never in a big rush to spend time with me and my car.

Calling a gas station for help was even worse. Some of the most uncomfortable moments in my life have been spent standing in a lovers' lane listening to a mechanic make obscene remarks about the situation as he poked around under the hood of my car. I would watch the yellow emergency light atop the tow truck scan, every three seconds, the interiors of all the cars parked in the lovers' lane and feel the unseen eyes of my fellow lovers'-laners seething through me with rage. Laura would sit with her back to the door, hoping that no one would recognize her.

On numerous occasions when my car didn't start, I became so desperate I prayed to St. Jude, the patron saint of hopeless cases. But usually my car was even too hopeless for him.

With my car, I couldn't even park on side streets with Laura. I'd no sooner turn off the engine than a cop would be at my window telling me I'd have to more along because some old lady had called, complaining about a strange car parked in front of her house and some people in the car acting peculiar. I used to see those old ladies peeking through their Venetian blinds, trying to get their cheap thrills. Yet not once did I ever call the police department and complain about a strange house parked in front of my car and some old lady in the house acting peculiar.

Eventually I had to completely give up the game of parking and petting. I was even beginning to hallucinate that my car would learn to talk and threaten to expose me to the world as a sex fiend unless I bought it new headlights and a set of snow tires.

For two years that car and I sputtered along together. And during those years I discovered what Crazy Freddie had known all along. My car was a born killer.

In the winter my car would try to starve me to death financially by using more antifreeze than gas. Its heater would never work except late at night when I was tired. Then it would try to "dry heat" me to sleep. In summer the radiator would let off steam every two blocks.

On turns, the steering wheel would struggle to shimmy out of my hands, the windshield wipers failed only if the snow was sticking, and tires went flat in the middle of railroad tracks.

But my life was gradually changing. I was no longer that interested in the White Sox's chances for a pennant. Instead of ordering gas a dollar at a time, I was now casually telling the attendant to "fill 'er up."

One day, the gas station attendant asked me when I had last changed the oil.

"Oil? I never knew you changed oil."

"You do," he said, "and you'd better."

So I did, which was the beginning of the end. The new blood was too rich for my car's old veins. I came home late one night. When I went out to my car in the morning, it was moaning much louder than usual from the previous night's efforts. It never ran again for me.

I sold the car for a dollar to a kid down the street. I got the better of the deal. Together, we pushed it along until it was in front of his house.

A few days later I went out and bought a "new" car. It was only two years old. After parking it in front of the house, I was about to head up the front steps when I looked down the street and saw my old car still huddled along the curb, in the same spot that I and its new owner had pushed it. I turned and walked down the street to where the old car stood, debated a moment, and then decided to hop in just to see how it would feel.

Already it had slipped into senility. Unlike the petite steering wheel in my nifty new car, the old steering wheel felt large and clumsy in my hands The pedals were stiff and cumbersome. The seat felt awkward and dirty. I even forgot to punch the door to get out.

A few months ago I was driving along a superhighway, which really wasn't so super, on a sun-soaked summer afternoon. The day was so hot that if I listened carefully I could hear my twelve-belted, wide-track, four-ply polypowered tires gasping as they continually retched themselves free from the asphalt. Although the world around me was swimming in sweat, there wasn't a drop of perspiration on my brow. My twenty-four-hour deodorant still had fourteen hours to go, the camel hair sport coat was hanging glibly in the back seat, and the car's air conditioner was keeping the atmosphere at a steady seventy-six degrees.

Like bored sentries, my eyes lazily scanned the rearview mirror and then casually shifted direction to observe the reflections in the sideview mirror. That's when I saw it: a four-wheel glob of dull blue steel hobbling along a few hundred feet behind me in an adjoining lane—a sibling of my first car.

I eased my foot off the gas pedal, allowing the sibling

to gain on me. Within seconds I got a good look at it as it pulled abreast of me and began crawling by. The metal around its headlights was rusted through. The side-vent window on the passenger's side was cracked. A piece of rope held down a trunk that was permanently ajar. The engine wheezed sporadically as it struggled to stay alive.

There was a young man at the steering wheel. Beside him, right beside him, was his girlfriend. She was laughing about something and he was nodding in agreement.

My car was worth at least thirty times more than his. I had little worry of my car overheating or stalling and absolutely no fear of its falling apart. With his car, he did. Yet it was I, at least at that moment, who would have liked to trade places with him.

I stepped on the gas and powered past the old blue car, which quickly melted into a dot within my sideview mirror. Remembering the words that I had spoken to Laura, only now realizing that they were referring, not to a car but to the young years of our lives.

"Enter into the kingdom that has been prepared for you for all eternity."

13

Watching Lanner empty out his locker. Tom and I had come to school early that morning. He didn't want to meet anyone.

It only took a few minutes. All the books fit into his school bag. The stragglers, such as the pencils with the broken tips, lunch bags he had forgotten about, the metal rocket left over from the science project, and the sweater with most of its buttons missing, he either pushed into the crevices of the school bag or stuck in his pockets.

A month before, Lanner had told me he was leaving. After two and a half years at Bremmer he couldn't afford the tuition anymore. He was transferring to McKinley Public High School.

There was nothing wrong with going to a public high school. Every year a few guys would transfer out of Bremmer to attend one just because they were fed up with Bremmer. But that was different. They wanted to go.

When I was a little kid, the closest I got to a public school was on various saints' days, which we had off and the public schools didn't. Along with some of my friends, I would stand in the public-school playground and yell "suckers" up at the windows.

Throughout my school years the nuns and priests informed us that we were privileged to be allowed to attend a Catholic school and that, if we goofed off too much, we could be sent over to the public school where "they have to take you. They have to take everybody."

When I was in seventh grade, I had a friend whose father was the janitor at a public school a few miles away from my neighborhood. One Saturday morning his father took us to work with him. The halls of the public school were much darker and colder than I had thought they would be. Everything looked old, or at least different. Some of the walls were marred with scribblings. It looked just like the kind of place that had to take everybody.

Whenever a public-school kid transferred to the Catholic school he was automatically put back a grade. That was done because a Catholic school supposedly did a much better job of teaching its students. It may have. Whenever a Catholic and a public school took the same achievement tests, the Catholic school beat the public school's brains out.

I didn't think about it much during the month that I knew Lanner was leaving. There was no point. Why get worked up over something that I could do nothing about? I'd still see him, I'd still hang around with him. But it would be different.

If Lanner had been the type that made noise—an athlete, a school-spirit nut, or even a loudmouth, poor-but-proud type—someone at Bremmer would have figured out a way to keep him.

Even as I watched Lanner clean out his locker, I kept

imagining Brother Purity coming around the corner to the rescue.

"What's going on here?" he'd ask.

"I'm transferring to a public school, Brother," Lanner would reply, "because I haven't got the money to stay here at Bremmer."

"You put your things back in your locker," Brother Purity would say. "You think we'd let a nice guy like you leave our fine school just because he didn't have enough money?"

The first-period bell had already rung. A few feet down the hall from Lanner's locker a class was saying its morning prayers. Tom tried to quietly close the locker door but the locker, now empty, belched out a hollow rattle.

That afternoon my class was kept late by Brother Forleau, our English teacher, because one of us had made a noise and Brother Forleau couldn't figure out who it was. Since no one would turn squealer, Brother Forleau made the whole class stay after school. Mass retaliation was a typical teacher practice.

After Brother Forleau released us, I went back to Tom's locker to make sure it was still clean. At Bremmer lockers left unlocked quickly became splattered with used notebook paper and other debris. I didn't want that happening to Lanner's locker. I found only one crumpled paper.

Walking toward the main exit. Wondering what Brother Purity and the others like him did on saint's days when they were kids.

"Suckers."

14

LATE BLOOMER

Six months before I was due to graduate, my homeroom teacher told me to report to the guidance counselor. It was school policy that everyone, before the end of his senior year, had to see the guidance counselor. Otherwise, the school administration feared, the student might do something worthwhile with his life.

Brother O'Connell, the guidance counselor, was a suave and contented fellow and had every reason to be. The other faculty members had to handle forty slobs an hour. He took them one at a time. Brother O'Connell had the soft job of being guidance counselor because a few years earlier, while teaching at a school in New York, he went berserk in class and tried to throw a kid out of a third-floor window. The kid lived through the attack only because the rest of his class convinced Brother O'Connell that it would be better to go up to the fourth floor since some people have been known to live through third-floor falls. Of course, the students grabbed Brother O'Connell the second he moved away from the window to head up to the fourth floor. The Bremmer Religious Order had Brother O'Connell committed for a few years and then sent him to Bremmer High School as a guidance counselor.

For the safety of the students Brother O'Connell's office was located in the basement of the school. When I walked in he was looking at a folder that contained my permanent records. From Day One of first grade, I had been told that my permanent records contained everything about me from the Baptismal waters on my forehead to the locker handle I had broken this morning.

Brother O'Connell asked me what I was going to do after I graduated. Going to college, I told him. I really had no idea of what I was going to do, but I thought that was what he wanted to hear. I was wrong.

Brother O'Connell was amused by my reply. My permanent records must have informed him that I was graduating in the bottom fiftieth of my class, had a character development strongly resembling silly putty, and the attitude of a malignant tumor.

"Where?" he smilingly asked in that tone of voice one normally uses when addressing twelve-point I.Q.s.

"Norte Dame." I said it to be mean. First in the heart of every Irish brother or priest is Notre Dame. They love it more than apple pie, and for someone like me to have even mentioned the thought of attending it was pure blasphemy.

Brother O'Connell leaned back in his guidance counselor's swivel chair—swivel so that he could look out the basement window and be philosophical, which was what he did. Brother O'Connell began talking to the window.

"Don't be ridiculous. With these permanent records you could never get into Notre Dame."

Fine, I thought to myself, I'll leave the damn records here with you. I've never seen them anyway. I don't even know what's in them, although occasionally I've heard glimpses of what might be there. "Yes, yes, that would look good on your permanent records." "No, no, we couldn't do that. It would look bad on your permanent records." Those are as close as I've ever been to that folder, which supposedly exposes the very innards of my soul to any meandering adult who cares to know.

But I said nothing.

Brother O'Connell swiveled away from the window and flopped his fat flimsy arms down on the desk. The fingers of his hands interlocked as his thumbs began drawing imaginary circles around one another. *Thumb Raped in Guidance Counselor's Office. Suspect from the Left Hand Being Held.* One thinks strange thoughts in the guidance counselor's office.

I could tell that Brother O'Connell had just thought of the solution to the problem of what he should do with my life. Saliva began to drip from his lips. His voice dropped a dozen decibels and he began talking in a used-car salesman drawl.

"Have you ever thought of the army?" he asked.

Of course, I silently replied, I've thought of the army. Who hasn't had nightmares?

"No," I said, "I've never thought of the army."

"It would be good for you. You could learn a trade there, you know."

Now I knew I was in trouble. Dumb, I admit to being. Brainless, I am not. "Trade" was simply another name for work. Even I knew that.

Brother O'Connell read the reaction in my eyes, negative, and countered with the weapon of ultimate force, my permanent records. He eased the folder up from the desk with two pinched fingers as if it were used toilet paper.

"According to your permanent records, Eddie," first

211

name, we were buddies now, "you don't seem to be college material."

College material! I shout to myself. Look, sickie, I've just left a room full of bloated, acne-stained, profanity-polluted, booze-bound, sex-sick penny loafers slobs. Most of them are college material. Not me, man—I'm going to work for a living.

"You're right," I said, and the conference was over. Brother O'Connell relaxed back in his swivel chair, content with the life he had chosen for me. With my lack of intelligence, he probably figured, in no time I'd be a general.

I sat out the rest of the day in a daze, which was the way I passed through most of high school. But immediately after school I went looking for help in the form of Timmy Heidi.

Two nights later he and I were sitting at my dining room table, which was cluttered with college brochures and application forms. Heidi was scanning my high school grade reports. Some people keep whips around to punish themselves. Others use religious artifacts. I kept my high school grade reports.

"These are absolute shit."

"I know that, Heidi, I know that."

"Obviously, your grades aren't going to get you into college," he said. "But sometimes a college will let you in if you can show that you've been active in school and community activities." Ready to write, Heidi laid his pen hand on a pad of paper. "What extracurricular activities have you belonged to at school?"

"None."

"None?"

"Well, I was on the varsity bowling team for two

weeks and I was a hall guard for three days before I got canned."

"What happened? Someone stole your hall?"

"Cut the crap, will you, Heidi?"

"Sorry. How about community groups?"

"Nope."

"You were a cub scout, weren't you?"

"Yeah, that's right."

"I'll put that down," said Heidi. "It can't hurt. Did you get any important awards?"

"I didn't get any awards."

"You didn't get any awards? How long were you a scout?"

"Two years."

"And you didn't get any awards at all?"

"No." I could tell that even Heidi found it difficult to believe that I could have existed for so long in an organization that gave medals for everything from inventing nuclear weapons to excellence in toilet training and still have emerged with my blandness unblemished.

"How about letters of recommendation?" asked Heidi. "Is there anyone you know who would write a letter stating that although you've been a jerk up to this point, you show signs of growing up? You know, the 'late bloomer' jazz."

"My father, if I've just cut the lawn."

"No, you asshole, I mean somebody who counts, like a teacher at school."

"No, I guess not."

"It's getting late," said Heidi. "I've got to get home. Here, sign these five applications and I'll fill them out and mail them for you."

"Thanks a lot for all the help," I said as I signed them.

"Some help," Heidi replied as he stuck the applications in his coat pocket. "I've got to think of an angle or you've had it."

Three days later, as we sat eating lunch in the cafeteria, Heidi informed me that he had mailed out the five applications that morning. "I think that at least one of them will accept you."

"Why?"

"Because I sent a letter with each application explaining that you were a member of a minority group."

"Minority group?"

"Yeah, colleges are becoming very self-conscious about not having members of minority groups."

"Heidi, I'm not a member of any minority group."

"Yes, you are. In the world of higher education, where everyone's a smart guy, you, Ryan, are a dummy."

Within three weeks I had received letters of rejection from four colleges. Only my sister and I were home on the day the fifth reply came. It was a letter of acceptance from Sabina College. Running to tell my older sister, who was ironing in the kitchen.

"I've just been accepted into college."

"Where at?" She put down the iron.

"Sabina College."

"Sabina? The one in Wisconsin?"

"Yeah, that's the one."

She picked up the iron again. "You jerk, that's an all-girl school."

I looked down at the torn envelope, which was still in my hand. It was addressed to "Edie Ryan."

214

15

THE JOLLY SEASON

I love Christmas, in the summer. Walking down a simmering sidewalk on an August afternoon, the sun hammering down on my head hoping to shove me through the sidewalk, a Christmas song will begin serenading my mind and the idea of Christmas will feel very cozy to me. But when the real thing comes crawling across the calendar, it never seems that appealing.

I've always found the Christmas season hard to take. From Thanksgiving day on, you're suppose to be delirious with joy just because Christmas is coming. If you're not, you start thinking that something's wrong with you. Eventually you end up getting depressed just because you're not extremely happy.

The holiday season was toughest on me when I was a kid. Even after I had dropped out of the Santa Claus faith, my world continued to revolve around that red-green ball of Christmas whose glow, no matter how distant, could be seen from every day of the year.

About a month before, like the flirt that it was, Christmas would slyly start becoming suggestive. Holiday songs drifted onto the air waves. Salvation Army bells bonged from every street corner while strings of colored lights littered the neighborhood as they snaked across storefronts, looped along ceilings, lined doorways, and ran around light posts.

In school, strips of silver tinsel would pop up across the edges of the bulletin boards, blackboards, doorways, and a few students who didn't move fast enough when the nun was running around with her staple gun putting the stuff up. Art classes were devoted to drawing and coloring such seasonal scenes as the Three Wise Men and the Nativity scene. At the classroom's Christmas party, at least one kid would try to asphyxiate himself on a popcorn ball. Gifts that emerged from the grab bag would unravel previously unknown dimensions of the "fifty cents and under" world.

When Christmas was within days of happening, my mother would make hundreds of her Christmas cookies. They were superb if you ate them within seconds after they came out of the oven. If, however, you delayed consuming them for only a few minutes, they would stale and were as hard as stone.

Besides dropping hints to my parents about what I wanted to see under the tree, I spent the days preceding the big event trying not to think about it so that it would come faster. But Christmas was not so easily conned. The more determined I became not to think about it, the more often I did.

When Christmas finally did decide to arrive, it only stayed twenty-four hours. That never made sense to me. I'd have said to myself "Gee, today really is Christmas" only a few times when it would be over. After all those days of working and waiting, it should have lived at least a week.

The worst thing about Christmas was that it was followed by the "day after." From at least the middle of

November my anticipation for Chrismas pumped up by the helium of hope, would float higher and higher. But the "day after" was twenty-four hours of fizzle. The new toys were already a bore. My imagination had been playing with them for well over a month. Colored bulbs would begin dying along the string of lights that rimmed the living room windowsill. The leftover turkey would give up its moisture, the tree its needles, and me my mind. There were no dreams on the "day after," but only the corpse of the Christmas spirit that had lived the day before.

Naturally, as I grew older, I didn't get as high as I used to for Chrismas, which meant that I didn't have as far to fall on the day after. So in senior year I wasn't expecting to fall farther on the day after than I ever had before.

On the last day of school before the holiday vacation, the student body of Bremmer High School had to attend the annual glee-club concert that was held in the school gym. Although many of the guys hated to go, I looked forward to it. I've always liked the way glee clubs sound and the songs they usually choose to sing. Occasionally the members of the Bremmer Glee Club would wail out an eerie Latin chant that would make you want to look for the candles and the open coffin. But most of their songs were pretty good. I really liked listening to them even though, like every simple-looking Bremmer student, I did my damnedest to avoid joining them.

The glee club was the only extracurricular activity in the school that drafted its members. You'd be sitting in class on an early autumn day, gracefully going through the motions, when you'd look up and see Brother Raffling, the glee-club director, standing in the doorway. He

217

would scamper through the rows of desks pointing his finger at various victims. "You, you, and you, line up in the hall. You, you, and you, join them. You, you, and you...."

Though he could force students to join the glee club, Brother Raffling realized that he couldn't keep anyone in it against his will. Therefore Brother Raffling tried to choose for his auditions those who looked too simple-minded to quit the glee club once they had been sucked in. I was always chosen.

In one long strand we would wait along the wall outside of Brother Raffling's small office. Each of us would then be called in to stand next to Brother Raffling's piano. He would strike numerous notes on the keyboard and tell the auditioning student to hum along. If someone made a mistake of sounding even faintly human, he was in.

Brother Raffling never bothered going after freshmen. Too many of their voices were still changing. There was nothing in life more aggravating for a glee-club director than to discover in the middle of a concert that one of his altos had, in the past few hours, became a bass.

In sophomore year the student standing in front of me in the glee-club audition line was a senior named Benjamin Franzel. Benjamin told me that when Brother Raffling asked me to hum along, rather than releasing all the air in my lungs through my mouth I should instead drop half of the air down along the back wall of my throat, returning it to my lungs. They would, in turn, bop my stomach into my bowels. If performed properly, said Benjamin Franzel, the resulting racket would be more than enough to keep me out of the glee club.

At my audition Brother Raffling hit notes on the piano

and I hummed along in precisely the style I had just been taught by Benjamin Franzel. As I was groveling through one of the bass notes, Brother Raffling interrupted me. "Have you ever had your throat operated on?"

"No, Brother."

"You should have."

In my senior year, on that Friday before the three-week holiday break, the glee club performed superbly. They sang all the Christmas standards, a number of currently popular songs, and finished up with a flurry of college school songs. The entire performance was marred by only one very brief Latin chant.

We were released from school two hours early that afternoon because the gym had to be converted from a glee-club concert hall back to a gym. At the beginning of the holiday season Bremmer High School traditionally hosted a basketball tournament. Being the perfect host, Bremmer always lost the first game.

It appeared as if the format would remain unchanged that evening. We were scheduled to play St. Beatrice, that little, all-Black, mostly girls, high school. St. Beatrice was the same school that Bremmer, during every football season, loved to chew and spit out. During the basketball season, though, it was St. Beatrice's turn to chew and spit. The school had only seven players on its team, but that was six more than it needed to beat Bremmer.

The most exciting moments of a Bremmer High School basketball game came when the teams were in their locker rooms. It was during half time that the Bremmer Tumbling Team performed.

Most athletic teams produced by Bremmer High School were about as gutsy as a bowl of Pablum. Not the tumbling team. The only difference between a demolition derby and a Bremmer tumbling-team performance was that the tumblers didn't bother hiding in cars.

Bremmer was the only Catholic high school in the city with a tumbling team. But then Bremmer was also the only school that had a Brother Sens, who was the coach of the tumbling team.

All the tumblers were as small as Brother Sens with the exception of Timmy Heidi, who was over six feet tall. Heidi was among the better tumblers on the team.

During the tumbling team's daily practice sessions Brother Sens, who was seventy years old at the time, would mention to his tumblers that he felt he had lived long enough. He would also inform them that he thought they, too, had lived long enough.

"Believe me, boys," Brother Sens would say with that smiling sneer stretched across his little face, "everything interesting in my life occurred in the first few years of it. The last fifty-sixty years have been a bore. If anything worthwhile was going to happen to you guys, it would have happened by now. The rest of your lives are going to be a drag; so you might as well live dangerously." They did.

At half time it would take some eye adjustment for the spectators to go from watching six-foot-plus basketball players to seeing a group of tumblers who looked like they had been born on the same cookie sheet. For the first three minutes of their performance, you kept waiting for the other half of their bodies to show up.

As the long narrow row of mats was placed on the floor, along with a small, stool-like trampoline, a few of the tumblers would warm up the crowd by doing handstands, cartwheels, and other tumbling tidbits. Once the equipment was set up, the newer members of the tumbling team would execute various acrobatic stunts, such as aerial somersaults and stationary mobiles. Nothing too impressive.

With less than five minutes remaining in the half-time intermission, the tumblers would finally get down to serious business. Those in the crowd who had been through it before would check their fingernail supply to make sure they could endure the ordeal without drawing their own blood.

The four best tumblers on the team, including Timmy Heidi, would stand along the far wall while, in the middle of the gym floor, the remaining tumblers would stand adjacent to the mat. When Brother Sens gave the signal, certain tumblers would kneel down on the mat and atop each other to form a human pyramid. The crash course was ready.

Separately, the four tumblers standing along the wall would sprint across the floor, pounce onto the trampoline, spring off, and dive over the human pyramid, their shirts literally skimming the back of the high man. The tumbler would land in a somersault roll, jump to his feet, and be promptly rewarded with a crowd-clapping ego massage.

After all four tumblers had cleared it, additional members of the tumbling team would attach themselves to the pyramid, building it even higher. The procedure would continue until every member of the tumbling team, with the exception of the four who were making the dives, was in the pyramid. By then that human triangle of flesh would seem too high for anyone to fly over it. Yet, incredibly, each of the four tumblers would continue to run, bounce, and sail over the pyramid, by now clearing the top man so closely that you could almost hear their skins squeak.

Occasionally a tumbler would fail to make it, skipping off an upper layer of his teammates. If he collided directly with the human pyramid, the entire structure would collapse into a tangle of arms and legs. When that occurred a few heads opened up. But as Brother Sens often told his tumblers, when it came to other people's heads his courage knew no limits. His tumblers would simply untangle themselves and start all over again.

The beginnings of that Friday night went as expected. Tom Lanner, Felix Lindor, and I arrived at the gym about forty-five minutes before the game to be sure of finding seats in one of the front rows. A sock hop was scheduled to be held after the game so we knew there'd be a large crowd competing for the seats. By half time St. Beatrice was bashing Bremmer 41 to 12. The Bremmer players were so far out of it that most of the time they were even on the wrong end of the court.

During the intermission the tumbling team did its usual flashy job of dazzling everyone who watched. Timmy Heidi especially seemed to be in excellent form. The higher the pyramid grew, the more gracefully Heidi floated over it. Until he made his final run.

There was less than a minute left of the half-time intermission. The pyramid was at its maximum growth. Heidi pushed off from the far wall, his long legs lunging across the floor as he loped toward that triangle of teammates. He jumped onto the small trampoline, ricocheted off perfectly, and, with his body horizontal to the gym floor, calmly cruised over the pyramid. But his landing could have been better.

Heidi went into his landing somersault later than he should have. He bounced up awkwardly from the mat and inadvertently dropped all his weight on the edge of his foot. What most people's memories later magnified into an obscene crackle rifled through the gym as the bone in Heidi's leg broke, leaving him to crumple softly to the floor. At least six girls around me headed straight for vomitsville. Tom Lanner's mouth hung open and he began breathing heavy and deliberate.

"Not you, too, Lanner," I said. "If you're gonna get sick, get the hell out of here."

"I'm not getting sick. But I think I'll go to the washroom anyway. I gotta take a piss."

"Yeah, yeah, just go." I'd make a lousy doctor. I looked over at Felix Lindor.

"Don't worry about me, Ryan," he said. "The only time I had the urge to throw up tonight was when I was watching the basketball game."

That kind of thing, like Heidi breaking his leg, never bothered me as long as I didn't think about it. I avoided thinking about it that night by faking an interest in the stomach stabilities of Lanner and Felix Lindor.

Heidi was carried off the gym floor on a stretcher to a station wagon, which had been pulled up to the front doors of the gym. He seemed to be in a fair amount of pain. Just as they were moving him through the doors, everybody stood up and gave him a standing ovation. Heidi, whose head was swelling faster than his broken leg, tried to wave to the crowd and in the process almost threw himself off the stretcher.

I had been in a crummy mood until Heidi had managed to mangle himself. Two weeks earlier, Una and I, after having another one of our arguments, had decided to stop seeing one another. Actually she had decided. I don't even remember what it was about. Since we argued over everything, it's difficult to recall one specific incident.

I really felt bad about having the fight with her. She had only been home a day after having been in the hospital a week for an appendix operation. I couldn't go up to see her because I had the flu that same week. Every day that Una was in there, though, I had called her on the phone.

On her last night in the hospital I asked Una to my Christmas dance, which was to be held on the day after Christmas. We spent more than an hour on the phone discussing the dance; who we were going to double with, what kind of corsage Una would like, where we planned on eating afterward. The argument came the next day when there was no longer a phone line between us. I hadn't talked to Una since then.

Except for the senior prom the Bremmer Christmas dance was the biggest social event of the year. If you were dating a girl regularly, then of course you took her. If, however, you were, as they say, playing the field, then you would try to find a girl whose looks and social standing would impress the hell out of everybody.

But with the Christmas dance now less than two weeks away, most of the decent bodies, much less the fabulous ones, had long since been put on reserve. All that remained were the general-circulation girls and you didn't take one of those to a Christmas dance.

Nevertheless, I was still clinging to the infinitesimal possibility of meeting, at the post-game sock hop, an available female of Christmas-dance quality. Even if I did meet such a girl, though, I knew that she probably wouldn't accept my invitation. Christmas-dance girls don't go for guys of Halloween caliber. But the moment that Heidi fractured his fibula or whatever it was, I knew I had a chance.

Although he wasn't even present, Heidi was the major celebrity of the sock hop. Considering how the basketball game had gone, there wasn't much else to talk about except Heidi and his broken leg. Since Lanner, Felix Lindor, and I were all close friends of Heidi, we instantly became minor celebrities. The sock hop had hardly begun when some girl walked up to Felix Lindor and started a conversation with him about Heidi's accident. A small but enthusastic group was beginning to gather around Lanner, and people I hardly knew were walking by me and saying hello. Normally that never happened. People I knew *well* often didn't bother saying hello to me.

Shortly after the sock hop began I saw a shoulder, followed by the body of Yvonne Yatsen shoving its way through the gym-floor congestion. Yvonne Yatsen was a fat and ugly girl who always attended such affairs with Monica Radil. Both of them went to St. Elizabeth High School, which was the same school that Una attended.

Monica Radil was extremely attractive, popular, and an honors student. Despite all of this she was a somewhat pleasant person. Monica was "going" with Gerald Lang, a sophomore at Illinois State University. That put Monica out of my league. I was doing well if I could compete socially with other high school hucksters like myself There was no way that I could contend with a college kid.

"Hi, Yvonne, how have you been?" I asked her as she nudged her big body past me. Not that I cared. But it was a safe enough question. Yvonne wasn't the type who would bother telling you. She figured that just by looking at her you already knew.

"Okay," she replied. "Isn't that terrible about Tim? I certainly hope that he's going to be all right."

"Yeah, I'm sure he will be. How's your friend Monica?"

"She's a little down tonight. She broke up with Gerry last week."

"Gerry?" I asked. "Is he the college boy she was going out with?"

"Yes, that's right. It's really too bad. I thought they were made for each other."

"Yeah, it's a real shame. Say, is Monica here with you?"

"Yes, she's right over there." Yvonne rocked her head slightly backward to indicate the direction. "That's where I'm going now."

"Hey, I'll come along with you and cheer up old Monica."

"That would be nice."

Monica didn't bother saying hello when she saw me but started right in about Heidi, asking me a billion questions about his broken leg. That night it was the thing to do. Monica always did what should be done.

I went into this very elaborate, and totally nonsensical, analysis of how Heidi went about breaking it. "He came out of his somersault roll somewhat prematurely," I said, enriching my presentation with hand gestures, "so that when he landed on his feet, his weight shifted sideways instead of forward so that when he tried to compensate. . . ." While I was throwing out this bullshit,

Monica just stared at me with this very serious look as if she were listening to a report on her own autopsy.

After that I started kidding around with her and Yvonne, telling them some jokes that I had recently heard, making cheap remarks about this teacher I had at the time, that kind of stuff. Yvonne wasn't too amused but Monica was, at least slightly. Her face maintained a pattern of deliberate smiles and calculated giggles.

When a slow song began playing over the public address system, I asked Monica to dance. She attempted to say something about how she couldn't leave Yvonne alone, but I interrupted her. "You don't mind if we dance for a few minutes, do you, Yvonne?"

"Oh, no, of course not."

What else could she say? It was an ignorant thing for me to do, but it was the only way I could talk to Monica alone.

With hundreds of others, our white socks padded across the gym floor. After glibly executing a one-liner, I waited for a lull in Monica's giggle. When it came, my mouth jumped in and asked her to my Christmas dance.

As planned, I had caught Monica's mind lounging in its laughter room. When the question of going to the dance, a strictly business matter, suddenly zinged in on it, Monica's mind tried to run back to its business office, where there was the proper atmosphere to make such a decision, but it just didn't have the time.

"Why certainly, Eddie. Sure. Yes, I mean, I'd like to."

As soon as the music stopped. I told Monica that I had to go look for Lanner and that I'd call her in about a week to give her the details on the dance. I had no desire to stand around and watch Monica sober up as she realized what she had done.

After the dance I met Lanner and Felix Lindor outside the front doors of the gym. There were piles of people waiting at the bus stop. I hate lines. It's never made much sense to me to stand in line and wait around just to give somebody my money. For December it was a decent night: fairly warm and covered by a sky that held little desire to lob anything earthward. The three of us lived only about two miles from school.

"You wanna walk home?" I suggested. "With that crowd we could be halfway there by the time we got on the bus."

"Okay," said Felix. Lanner nodded his agreement. Walking through the residential streets. Tombstones, in the forms of houses, stood rigidly behind patches of lawn, waiting for the sunrise that would trigger their resurrection.

"Man, what a sock hop," said Felix Lindor. "All night, girls kept coming up and asking me about Heidi. I got five dates with four different girls. God only knows how well I would have done if Heidi had broken both of his legs."

The night had not been so kind to Lanner. Rita Esbel, who had a boring body and a mind to match, had asked him to her school's Christmas dance. She attended St. Regis Catholic High School for girls. Although Rita got excellent grades, outside the classroom she had no idea what was going on. When a friend of hers asked her if she thought engaged girls should go all the way, Rita asked, "Where?"

Tom didn't date much. He couldn't afford it and he didn't seem to like it that much anyway. But even though he didn't want to attend her Christmas dance, he still said "yes" to Rita Esbel. Lanner found it very difficult to pronounce the word "no."

Unless you really liked the girl, going to a Catholic girl's school dance wasn't worth the effort. Your date would spend most of the night introducing you to everyone she knew, even vaguely. You didn't have to look very far past the "nice to meet you" and the synthetic smile to see the true thought fermenting behind most of their eyes. "So this is the twerp she talked about so much at the lunch table."

The nuns would spend all night weaving across the dance floor, making sure that none of the girls were dancing "suggestively," that is, moving anything above their ankles. The nuns also gawked around constantly looking for girls who, while dancing, were not maintaining "proper distance" between themselves and their dates. The "proper distance," according to the nuns, was a phone book away. They must have been referring to a world phone book because a girl started getting steaming stares from the nuns if she was close enough to her dancing partner to see the expression on his face.

At one of the girls' school's Christmas dances, Felix Lindor was repeatedly warned by one of the nuns that he was dancing too closely to his date. "Not less than five minutes ago," said the nun, "I told you that you must dance a phone book away from your partner."

"Oh," said Felix, "I thought you said a phone number away."

Walking into our neighborhood, I was still ecstatic over having maneuvered Monica into accepting my invitation to the Christmas dance. But not until Felix Lindor had left us to turn down his own street did I say anything about it to Lanner. I didn't feel like listening to a Felix Lindor analysis of Monica's anatomy.

"Hey, Tom, guess who I asked to the Christmas dance?"

"Who?"

"Monica Radil."

"Yeah?"

"'Yeah?' Is that all you've got to say, Lanner? She's one of the sharpest girls around." I shouldn't have expected much enthusiasm from Lanner. He was a big fan of Una's.

"How come you didn't ask Una?" Tom said.

"You know why I didn't ask her. I haven't even talked to her for a couple of weeks. We just don't get along, that's all. If you're so crazy about her, why don't you ask her out?"

"No, she's just a friend. That's all. Besides, I'd never date a girl you were going with."

"For Christ's sake, Lanner, I'm not going with her. I just told you that."

"Yeah, I know, I know."

On Christmas Day night, God decided to belatedly answer the prayers of the romantics and dumped five inches of snow on the city. In my neighborhood everything but the sidewalks shriveled up from the snow. Streetlights shortened as they recoiled from the winter sky. Cars with dual mufflers under the bumpers, "64,000" on the odometers, and "V8" engines in their chests shrank in humility as their wheels sputtered through the white slop. A person even seemed smaller as he walked through the streets. His torso would lean timidly forward and his shoulders, sitting straight up in the sockets, would attempt to stabilize the body as it shook from the shivers of the swirling cold. But the more snow that fell on the sidewalks, the wider they got. Their growth became most apparent when you were still pushing the shovel across the concrete, searching for the edge.

Sitting on the basement stairs, having just finished shoveling the snow. Raw yellow light blared from the lone sixty-watt bulb that dangled a few feet over my head. The light scratched at my unguarded eyes, whose pupils were still swollen from the darkness outside. My body was buried beneath layers of winter clothes. The toes were just beginning to tingle as they revived to the heat of the basement. As I unzipped the jacket and unbuttoned the first of three sweaters that I had on, my mind casually retraced the nearly dead day that had just been Christmas.

It had been an all right one, which was all I could expect at my age. I had received a lot of nice gifts, all of them clothes. Not that I didn't like clothes. It was just that when they were wrapped for Christmas they made such light gifts. I have always preferred heavy presents. It's tough to find a pair of slacks that weighs four or five pounds.

Dissatisfied with the thoughts of a boring Christmas day, my mind began savoring the anticipation of the Christmas dance that was the following night.

My mother opened the kitchen door and shouted down the stairwell at me. "Telephone."

Already I knew it was a girl calling me. I could tell by the way my mother yelled "telephone." Whenever a girl called me, which was very rare, my mother would always say "telephone" three octaves higher than usual. It was her way of smugly informing me that part of my private social life was now being exposed to her gaze.

"I'll take it upstairs." I flipped off my boots, went up the basement stairs two at a time, walked through the first floor of the house, up the stairs, and through the darkened hall to my bedroom. Until a year ago it had been my parents' room. They hadn't bothered moving the extension phone, which now squatted on a small desk in a corner of my room, haloed by a tiny table lamp.

I sat down on the edge of the bed and picked up the phone. "I got it." A click on the line signaled that some-one had hung up the phone in the dining room.

"Hello?"

"Hello, Eddie. This is Monica."

"How are you?"

"I'm fine, Eddie. And you?"

"Okay. Ready for the dance tomorrow night?"

"That's the reason I'm calling. Do you know Gerry Lang?"

"No."

"Well, he goes to Illinois State University. I've been dating him for quite a while. He came in for the holi-days and today he asked me to wear his fraternity pin."

"Oh, congratulations." What could I say? Fuck you, you bitch. That's what I wanted to say.

"The thing is, I won't be able to go to the dance with you because, well, now that I'm pinned to Gerry, that wouldn't be very right, would it?"

"No, I guess not." It's difficult to defend your position when your body's turning numb.

"I just knew you'd understand. Thanks, Eddie, good-bye."

I said "good-bye" but I don't think she heard it. Flicking off the table lamp. Lying back on the bed, wishing it would snow some more.

The next day in the late afternoon I went and picked up the tuxedo and the corsage. There was no choice. Both had been paid for. That morning I had come to the conclusion that I had absolutely no desire to explain to anyone, least of all my family, what had happened. I decided that I would leave the house that evening just as if I were going to the Christmas dance. I would stay out a sufficient number of hours and then come home and make up some lies about how nice the evening had been.

As I stood in my bedroom trying to put on the black bow tie, I heard my father's voice in the living room below. "Seven-thirty. Anything good on?" My little sister said something in reply to him as she clicked on the television. I recognized the third voice as that of my Uncle Elmer, who was a bachelor and lived a few blocks away.

My little sister was the first to notice me as I came down the stairs.

"Oh, Eddie, you look just beautiful. I mean handsome. I've never seen you in a tuxedo before."

"Thanks."

"You look nice," my father said.

"Sharp, very sharp," my Uncle Elmer reiterated.

"Thanks."

My mother came in from the kitchen. "You look very handsome."

"Thanks, mom."

"Take a look at yourself in the mirror," she said.

"Naw, I'd rather not."

"Go ahead," she persisted.

I walked over and stood in front of the football field

mirror that hung above the couch. I didn't actually look at myself, though. I just stared up at the ceiling for a few seconds.

"See, now aren't you proud of the way you look?"

"Yeah, ma." I walked over to the guest closet, opened it, and began looking for my overcoat. "I gotta get moving. Its getting late. . . ."

"Wait a second," my mother interrupted, "you forgot your corsage and boutonniere." She walked into the kitchen and I could hear the refrigerator door rapidly opening and shutting. She returned with a large plastic-wrapped flower and a small carnation that she began pinning to my lapel.

"Don't bother with it now, ma. I can do it later myself."

"Stand still. It'll only take a second." With one deft motion of the straight pin, she stitched the carnation to the lapel of the tuxedo. "Now, have a good time."

"I will, ma." She walked back into the kitchen.

Uncle Elmer got up from the couch, took a five-dollar bill out of his pocket, and thrust it at me. "Here's an extra five, in case you run short."

"I won't run short, Uncle Elmer. I have enough money. Thanks anyway."

"Go ahead, take it. These are your fun years, you know."

"I know, Uncle Elmer, but. . . ."

"Take the money," my father interjected.

"You're only young once, you know," continued Uncle Elmer. "These fun years will never come again."

I took the five-dollar bill from Uncle Elmer's hand. A small price to kill the conversation.

"Thanks, Uncle Elmer."

"That's all right. Have a god time."

I grabbed for the front door. "I'll be seeing you, everybody."

"Where are you going?" my father asked me. "I thought you were doubling with Joe Rabo and that he was picking you up here?"

"He is, dad. I just thought that I'd wait out in front for him."

"Don't act crazy. It's only ten degrees outside. Sit down and relax. He'll beep for you. He always does."

I sat down on the couch for a few seconds and then jumped up. "That's him. I'll see you all later."

"I didn't hear anything," said my father.

"Yeah, I did, dad. That was him." I pulled open the front door. "Good-bye, everybody." A barrage of "good-byes" staggered after me through the door.

Sticking the plastic-wrapped corsage under my arm, I hung onto the railing as I eased myself down the front-porch steps, which were covered with a skin of slick, worn snow. Then I walked toward the nearest corner of the block in order to be out of view from my house as quickly as possible.

I thought that I'd go up to a group of stores that crowded around an intersection three blocks from my house. I could wander in and out of them until 9:30 or 10:00 and at least stay warm most of the time. I had no idea of how I was going to waste another three or four hours.

My route took me directly past Lanner's house. He must have seen me coming. As I passed by he opened the heavy front door, then the storm door, and stuck his head out from behind it. "Hey, Ryan, where are you goin'? Come here a minute."

I trotted up the stairs of his front porch and stood beside the partially opened door.

"I thought the Christmas dance was tonight."

"Yeah, it is."

"Aren't you goin'?"

"Sure. I'm on my way over to Spaulding Street. I'm doubling with Joe Rabo and he's picking me up there."

"Hey, man, you ought to have a good time tonight."

"Yeah, I will."

"Wanna come in and warm up a second?"

"Naw, I gotta get going. Thanks, anyway."

"Hey, did you hear about Una?"

"No."

"She's back in the hospital again. Went in two days before Christmas.

"What's it this time?"

"She got an infection from the appendix operation. Nothing serious, but I think she'll be in there a while."

"That's too bad," I said.

"Why don't you go visit her sometime or send her a card or something?" Lanner suggested.

"I told you that I'm not going with her anymore."

"You don't have to be going with a girl just to send her a 'get well' card."

"No. I guess not, Tom. Why don't you send her a card or call her?"

"I don't know. I'm not too good at that sort of thing. Maybe I will. I don't know."

"I've got to get going, Tom, or I'm going to be late. Besides, I'm freezing my ass off."

Lanner closed the storm door and then yelled through it. "Have a good time."

"I will."

236

Sitting on a nearly empty bus, searching through a frost-flavored window for a building with a neon sign reading "Victoria Hospital" pinned on its chest. Seeing the sign, I picked up the plastic-wrapped corsage, which I had placed on the seat next to me, yanked the cord overhead, and jumped into the two-step hole that guarded the back door. Just as the bus was beginning to pull back from the reins of the brakes, I flipped open the doors and jumped out.

Victoria Hospital was the big kid on the block. Its eighteen-story frame ran past its neighbors by at least ten stories. Within its U-shaped arms was a courtyard crammed with trees and park benches.

As I walked through its main doors and across the foyer toward the reception desk, an old man crept past me. Most of his body was buried beneath a long, over-sized black coat while the ends of him were wrapped up by a beak cap with pull-down ear muffs and unbuckled rubber boots. I thought to myself the kind of one-liner that Heidi probably would have flipped at me if he had been around. "Think we should ask that guy how his mother was tonight?"

I began laughing to myself as I stood before the unattended reception counter. Any other time I would have felt sorry for the old man, if for no other reason than he was old, so I knew I was slipping into a giddy mood. The hospital was much warmer than the bus had been. I took off my coat and flung it over my arm. A ploppy middle-aged nurse came from around a corner and stood behind the reception counter. It was evident by her cardboard face that the starch in her uniform had somehow managed to invade her veins. She stared first at me, then my tuxedo, and finally at the plastic-wrapped corsage, which I had placed on the counter.

"Yes?" she challenged.

"Uh, I'd like to know what room Una Fabges is in, please."

Miss Starch pulled out a broad black binder from beneath the counter, slapped it down on the countertop, and flipped through it. "Room 1729. Take one of the elevators over there to your right."

"Thank you." Seconds later I stood before an elevator watching the numbers alternately light and dim across its forehead.

Number one lit up. When the elevator opened, inside it was an old lady on a cart, lying totally flat, with a nurse standing beside her. The old lady's eyes were closed. I thought maybe she was dead. As the nurse wheeled her out of the elevator and past me, the old lady's eyes flickered open momentarily and looked straight up at me. Apparently unimpressed by what they saw, they drowsed back beneath their lids. As I rode the elevator I tried to figure out what the old lady thought of me, if she thought of me at all.

Room 1729 was at the end of the hall. Peeking around the doorway, I could see that it was a semiprivate room but that the bed nearest the door was vacant. A small lamp hovered over Bed Two, providing the room with a sharp fan of light. The head part of the bed was propped up. Una was sitting there with a book resting in her hands but she wasn't reading. She was just staring out the nearby window.

My giddiness of only a few minutes before, already stifled by the stare of the old lady on the cart, now dissolved completely into fright. There was nothing to be scared of, I knew that. But I was scared anyway. I self-analyzed the fear. It was from my being uncertain about how to act when in doubt. I got obnoxious.

"Hello there, sick girl."

"Eddie! What are you doing here tonight?"

"Visiting you. What else?"

"Do you always dress so formally when you visit someone in the hospital?"

"No, uh, no, you see, the Christmas dance is tonight and . . . uh, I'm supposed to pick up Monica Radil in about forty-five minutes. You know her, don't you?"

"Vaguely."

"Anyway, I have a few minutes to spare so I thought I'd stop up and see how you're doing."

I stroked my chin in a doctorly manner and stiffened up my voice to make the pronouncement. "You certainly don't look sick to me."

Una, however, refused to acknowledge my clumsy grab for humor. "I'm not. You look very nice in your tuxedo."

I stood beside her bed and slowly turned around, holding my tuxedo coat open. "Notice the silk lining and the Continental cut."

Una said it more emphatically this time. "It looks very nice. Can I smell the flower?"

I had forgotten that I still held the corsage in my hand. "You can't smell it. It's wrapped in plastic. But you can see it." I held the corsage out toward her.

"It's very pretty. I'm sure Monica will be very pleased with it."

I tossed my overcoat on a chair that was next to Una's bed and placed the corsage on top of the coat. Then I walked over to her window and looked out. Below, I could see the hospital courtyard and the trees with their naked limbs lined by strips of snow. Across the street glowed the lukewarm windows of a department store. City lights peeked through the darkness that lay beyond.

"This room has a nice view. Spend much time looking at it?"

"Oh, yes. I often sit here just looking out over the city."

" I can see where you would." I turned around to look at Una. "What do you think about?"

"Many things. It's difficult to put into words."

I turned back toward the window. "Yeah, I suppose so."

I could hear Una sliding out of bed, putting on her robe and slippers, and walking up to stand beside me. She was wearing those big pink fluffy slippers. On anybody else, they would have looked dumb. But I liked the way they looked on her. As she leaned lightly on the windowsill she didn't even glance at me. All of her attention was given to the view.

"The last time I was here in the hospital," Una began, "I sometimes couldn't sleep at night, so I'd go sit in the solarium, which is on the top floor. Up there you can see the entire city in every direction. I'd often meet this old man and we'd sit, enjoying the view, talking about different things."

"That doesn't sound like too much fun," I said, not sure myself whether I was trying to be funny or serious.

"Not exactly fun, but I enjoyed it."

"In what way?"

"Well, sometimes, he'd tell me how different the city looked when he was young. . . ."

"A lot less lights, I'd imagine."

". . . yes . . . a lot less lights. Occasionally, he'd point to a cluster of them and he'd tell me about a job he worked in that area or how he lived in that section of the city for a while."

"Like what?"

"Oh, he'd tell me about the things he'd done down there among those lights during the various ages of his life. 'Let's see,' he'd say, looking at his watch, 'it's a quarter after one, now. If I was five years old, I might be getting up to get a drink of water from the pump in the kitchen. See that big office building with the red flashing light atop it? That's where the neighborhood I grew up in used to be. Back then that area was almost a suburb. Hard to believe, isn't it? Now if I was twenty, you see that patch of black over there?'" Una pointed at a corner of the window.

"Yes," I said, as I thought how strange it was to hear the words of an old man through a young girl's voice.

"'That's where I'd be at this time of night, walking with some pretty young thing, doing all the living I could do. And if I was sixty, I'd probably be in somewhere among all those lights over there, sitting in my brown easy chair, listening to the radio and reading the paper.'"

"One night," said Una, "when the sky was so black that the brilliance of the city seemed to leap out at us, the old man told me that each person on earth was a human light. Strong and bright in our young years, we find it difficult to see the other lights. But as we grow old and our own brightness dims, we can, for the first time, truly see the world around us."

"I don't understand that," I said.

"Neither did I," replied Una, "so the old man got up and turned on the lights in the solarium."

"What happened?"

"Looking out, we could hardly see the lights of the city through the reflections of the solarium staring back at us."

Silence. My words leaped to fill it. "Old people are funny, you know. Not funny funny, but funny strange-like. When I was a kid, my grandmother and aunt would come over to visit all the time. My aunt was in her fifties and my grandmother must have been in her seventies. Sometimes my aunt would complain about her aches and pains and my grandmother would look at her and say, 'Oh, what I'd give to be fifty again.' At the time, I thought my grandmother was crazy. What the hell, I was only ten. When you're ten, everyone seems to be crazy. Maybe they are. Do you still see the old man around here?"

"No, I don't. I think he had cancer. I don't know where he is now." Una turned away from the window, took a few quick steps, and sat down on the end of her bed. "Say, shouldn't you get going? You wouldn't want to be late for Monica."

I pulled back my sleeve and looked at my watch as if I really gave a damn what time it was. "I've still got a lot of time. I bet you found that depressing when the old man talked that way."

"When he talked he never depressed me. But some-times, when he stopped talking and simply looked out at the city, he made me feel very sad."

I thought of moving away from the window and sit-ting on the bed next to Una. But I figured she wouldn't appreciate me doing something like that. Una wasn't the kind of girl you sat on a bed with, not even in a hospital room.

"The trouble with being old," I said as I leaned back on the windowsill, "is that you're always sick or worried about getting sick. I read an article about how eighty percent of all laxatives are bought by people over sixty-five. It must be lousy to reach an age where your major concern in life is irregularity. I had an older cousin who died last year. He was in his thirties. His wife went into mourning by buying a black Impala with the insurance money."

Una popped herself off the bed and stood before me. "That's terrible!"

"An Impala's a good car."

"You know what I mean."

I turned around and looked out the window again. "You know, in another five months I'll be out of high school. Five months, that's not very far off." Already, I could see that seat in the solarium waiting for me. And the mother of the young girl who would be sitting next to me was still a generation away from being born.

Una sat down on the bed again. "What do you plan on doing with your life, Eddie?"

"I don't know. After I get through with my 'fun years,' ... these are my fun years, you know. That's what my Uncle Elmer keeps telling me." I went into my cheap imitation of Uncle Elmer's voice. " 'These are the fun years, enjoy them while you can.' Am I enjoying them? Yes sireee, I'm enjoying them. Anyway, after I get through these fun years, I'll probably go out and conquer the world in one way or another. Set sales records for Mutual of Omaha. Something like that."

"You don't have a date with Monica for the dance tonight, do you?"

"Not exactly." I picked up the plastic-wrapped corsage from the chair and began fidgeting with it. "Until last night I had the date with her. But she called me up and broke it."

"Would you like to talk about what happened?"

"No, I don't think so."

Una sat up stiffly. "Okay, you don't have to tell me."

I hate that, when someone offers to be your father confessor but gets ticked off because you don't feel like going to confession.

"It was no big deal," I said emphatically. "There are forty thousand comedians in the United States today and most of them are out of work. Tonight I'm one of them."

"I'm sorry," Una said, "I didn't mean to. . . ."

"Don't worry about it. It's no big deal." The only thing worse than Una being mad at me was her feeling sorry for me. She was so good at feeling sorry for you that, after a while, you had a strong urge to kill her. Not actually kill her, of course, but to just get her out of the way. "It's only a Christmas dance," I said. "That's all. No big deal."

"I think it's a big deal," Una said. "If Monica made the date with you, unless there was an emergency of some sort she should have kept it." Una's mind always thought in terms of emergencies.

"Unfortunately," I said, "there was nothing signed so I can't get her for breach of promise. Don't worry about it. It's not that important. It's just a crummy Christmas dance."

"Did you know," said Una, "that I've never been to a major school dance."

"Never? Why not?"

"I've always been in the wrong place at the wrong time. Last year, for instance, when St. Elizabeth held its spring dance, a close friend of the family passed away in Akron, Ohio, and my family and I had to take the train out there for the funeral."

"That's too bad."

"I know things like that aren't very important to a boy, but they are to a girl. But as you say, it's no big deal. I'll live just as well." Una busied herself adjusting the pillow on her bed.

My head was operating like a washing machine that night. It had already run through the resigned, giddy, scared, obnoxious, depressed, and melancholy cycles. Now I could feel it clicking into the grandiose. I walked over to the chair and put the plastic-wrapped corsage down again on top of my coat. Then I turned and stood in front of Una.

"I, Eddie Ryan, self-appointed social director of Bremmer High School, hereby officially designate this hospital room, number. . . ." I couldn't remember the damn hospital room number. I ran over to the door, looked above it, and then hustled back to stand again in front of Una. ". . . hospital room number 1729, an auxiliary ballroom of the Bremmer Christmas dance." I switched on the radio next to her bed and slowly turned the dial, searching for a station with slow music. Within three notches I had found it. Reaching for Una's hand.

"May I have this dance?"

"Here? You're kidding?"

The radio began playing "Misty." The FCC was definitely on my side. "Ah, perfect," I said. "Self-appointed social directors never kid."

Una eased herself over the edge of the bed and guided her feet back into her slippers. Through "Misty," three commericals, and a few other songs I can't even remember, we held each other and pretended to dance.

Looking over Una's shoulder at the lights of the city, wondering what they held for me. The muscles in my arm, rigid with restraint, begged to be allowed to go from a strong hug to a crushing caress. But the mind refused. I wanted her to be thinking of me and not my squeeze.

Feeling her being so close to my existence. The radio was playing "Tis the season to be jolly, fa la la la la, la la la la. . . ." Somewhere among the "la's" we both came aware of the phone ringing, the match that ignited the mood into ashes.

"Excuse me," said Una. Her words came quietly. They were almost asleep. She walked over to the phone and picked up the receiver. "Hello? Tom. . . . Fine, and how have you been?" Her voice was beginning to wake up.

I guessed that it was Lanner. I didn't know for sure. I still don't because I never asked him. But I think it was. I was beginning to hate myself. I was the asshole who told him to call her. And I was beginning to hate him because, like an asshole, he did.

Walking over to the chair that held the corsage and my coat. "I'd better get going."

Una turned away from the phone. "You're leaving now?"

"Yeah, I've got a lot of things to do, you know." I put on my coat and started buttoning it up. "I'll be seeing you."

246

"See you." Una turned toward the window with the phone still in her hand. "Yes, Tom, I'm here. I'm sorry, could you repeat that?"

I picked up the plastic-wrapped corsage and began walking toward the door. Just as I was about to leave the room, I decided to do it. Gently retracing my steps across the tile floor to Una's bed, I placed the corsage on her pillow. A very schmaltzy thing to do, I must admit. But then at times I'm a very schmaltzy person.

Seventeen floors later, walking through the courtyard. Was Una looking down at me? Maybe, I thought, she was too high to see. Stopping. looking up through the tree branches at a yellow fleck of light that I hoped held her. Walking on, the tight snow squeaking beneath the weight of my feet, reluctantly listening to the lyrics of a song that refused to leave my mind. "Tis the season to be jolly, fa la la la la, la la la la. . . ."

on the edge of Lake Michigan and its theater was easily the... high school gym or auditorium. With one or...

16

My high school years were now within minutes of being over. The 368 bodies that made up the senior class of Bremmer High School were propped up in rigid rows of folding chairs that loomed across the stage of McCormick Place. A monstrous white marble convention center, McCormick Place sat like a washed-up bar of Ivory Soap on the edge of Lake Michigan. McCormick Place was new and its theater was easily three times as large as any high school gym or auditorium. With such a capacity for peacock parents, disinterested siblings, and unmarried aunts and uncles, the McCormick Place Theater quickly became the "in" spot for school graduations.

Our graduation was taking place at one o'clock on Sunday afternoon. Two hours earlier, from the same stage, Chicago City College had held its graduation ceremony. At four o'clock a north suburban high school district was scheduled to do likewise. McCormick Place was the "McDonald's" of graduations. "I'd like one principal, a valedictorian, small size, one bishop with a ring to kiss, and three hundred and sixty-eight seniors, easy on the tassels, to go."

Norman Floss was our valedictorian. I had gone all the way through grammar school and high school with

Norman. The only word I ever heard him say during those twelve years was "Hi." That was it. He never recited in class but just sat at his desk, his knees and lap set in ninety-degree turns, staring at the front of the room. If his eyes hadn't been open, you would have thought he was dead. Outside of class Norman always had his head sandwiched between the covers of a book. He was like a man who wore glasses. If Norman didn't have a book in his hands, you had trouble recognizing him.

Norman Floss was a very nice guy. He was just extremely quiet. On graduation day I discovered why. He didn't have anything to say. When Norman delivered his speech he spoke exactly like a book. You could almost hear the commas and periods. It was very strange. Although I paid very close attention to his speech, I didn't hear a word he said. Norman Floss spoke for three hours and seven minutes.

Brother Purity talked next. No matter what words he chose, he always said the same thing. The "rah rah" bit about loving your school. I didn't bother listening. I was too busy cutting and pasting various moments of senior year into my emotional scrapbook.

At the end of the first week we were given our school rings. From the day I had entered high school, those pieces of metal and glass had been the ultimate symbol of manhood. The ring looked out of place that first time I slipped it onto my finger. But I knew it belonged there. I was a man now, a high school senior.

As Brother Purity continued to blab away, I looked down at the ring on my finger. I was still impressed.

The prom. I tried not to think about it but it relentlessly wedged itself into my mind. Our class officers had decided that instead of holding it in a downtown hotel, which was the normal thing to do, we would have our prom in the gym. The class officers said that besides being cheaper, the gym was a more appropriate site for our prom since it was a part of our school.

The only problem was that the gym and the adjoining locker room reeked with the odor of sweaty crotches. The smell was especially bad because no one ever bothered taking his gym suit home to wash it. In addition a freshman would sometimes take over a gym locker and, instead of buying his own gym suit, would use the one that had been left behind by the graduating senior. Some jockstraps in the locker room were so old that if they had been bottles of wine they would have been worth fifty bucks apiece.

For six weeks before the prom, the gym and locker room were declared off limits to students. All doors and windows were left open with the hope of attracting fresh air. On the night of the prom, when the first couple walked into the gym, they didn't travel five feet before the corsage on the girl's chest wilted and died. They walked another five feet before she wilted and died.

That was also the night that quite a few guys heard their dates sing the national anthem of Catholic girlhood. "I'm Saving Myself for Marriage." Not me, though. I went with Una. We had our usual nightcap argument topped off with the familiar "Maybe we shouldn't see each other for a while."

The last hour on the last day of class, Brother Dapel, our homeroom teacher, knew he was standing on a piece of time that was destined to go into each one of our personal halls of fame. "You are going to be amazed," said Brother Dapel, "at how quickly life changes for you in the next few years. Things that are unimportant now are going to become very important. And much of that which you think important today will become insignificant in the future. For instance, during the past four years your fellow classmates have played a major role in your life. It's probably very important to you what most of the students in this room think of you. But in another four years you will have completely forgotten about most of the people in this room."

A few minutes later, walking out of class for the last time, Timmy Heidi turned around to me. "Brother Dapel was wrong about that."

"Wrong about what?"

"I've already forgotten about most of the people in this room."

Bishop Mandings was talking now. He was giving us the old garbage man routine. ". . . it doesn't matter what you choose to do in life. What does matter is how well you choose to do it. If you decide to be a garbage man, there's nothing wrong with that. Just make up your mind to be the best garbage man that you can possibly be." Mandings was just trying to show us that he thought all men were created equal, even though he knew they weren't. How many garbage men's rings had he kissed lately?

During my four years at Bremmer, numerous alumni had been invited back by Brother Purity to talk to us and show us what great successes they had become. Some of them were bankers, engineers, lawyers, and businessmen. But none of them picked up garbage for a living, although they were all quite good at delivering it.

The bishop was now thanking us for our senior gift to

Bremmer, the furniture in the faculty room. It had been there for five years.

Bishop Mandings finished his speech and returned to his seat at the front of the stage. Dressed in the red hat and flowing robes and holding his staff, Bishop Mandings's touch, even though it wasn't the most glorious part of him that did the touching, seemed to instantly turn the plain leather chair into a throne. He sat so that his profile faced both the graduates and the audience. Brother Purity then called out the names as a continuous line of seniors began flowing across the stage to stand in front of Bishop Mandings. He would hand each one a diploma and the new graduate would kneel and kiss the bishop's ring.

"John Abalis ... John Ahern ... Michael Anderson ...."

Michael Anderson, whose face always sat in a smile. A month into senior year, during the first few minutes of homeroom period, Brother Purity came to the door and asked to see Mike outside in the hall. Brother Purity was the man who came to get you when you were in big trouble. We knew, though, that there had to be some other reason for Brother Purity asking to see Michael Anderson. Mike didn't get into big trouble. Walking toward the front of the room, Mike milked the moment for what it was worth by slipping a textbook into the seat of his pants. It got some good laughs. A few hours later we were told that Mike's father had dropped dead five minutes after Mike had left the house. Before the year ended four more seniors would lose their fathers.

"... Donald Dobelis ... Anthony Donovan...."

Anthony Donovan who, throughout his high school years, got his sexual gratification from the rope hanging

253

in the gym. And on prom night showed up with a girl who looked just like the rope.

". . . Phillip Kalaski . . . William Kline . . . Ernest Kogan. . . ."

The Vietnam war was building up speed when Ernie went to the show one night and saw a typical John Wayne movie. The next day Ernie joined the marines. Less than a week after he landed in Vietnam, Ernie Kogan stepped on a land mine that blew off all his limbs. His parents picked him up from the airport in a basket. Thank you, John Wayne.

". . . Stanley Mitchell . . . James Moore . . . William Muley. . . ."

Billy Muley, a football player, who got his girlfriend pregnant. His friends tried to collect a dollar from each senior so that Billy could run off with his girl. Timmy Heidi contributed two dollars and told them to make sure Billy went twice as far.

". . . Bernard Pinzik . . . Bruce Porter. . . ."

Who, upon flunking out of college, became so upset that he tried to commit suicide by downing a bottle of sleeping pills. But in his haste Bruce grabbed a bottle of laxatives instead. Bruce didn't die. He only wished he had.

". . . Thomas Reynolds . . . Robert Riss . . . Mark Rodes . . . Edward Ryan. . . ."

Walking across the stage, accepting my diploma from Bishop Mandings. kneeling and kissing his ring and hoping the guy in front of me didn't have a communicable disease.

A few minutes later the ceremony ended. Now all that remained of the graduating class of Bremmer High School was a 155-page yearbook and a metal plaque in

254

the faculty room. Still dressed in cap and gown it took me at least ten minutes to find my family in the lobby. It had sounded so simple when we planned it at home. "Eddie, we'll meet you in the lobby right after the ceremony." "Okay, Dad." It had probably sounded just as simple for the other 367 graduates and their families who had agreed on the same place for their rendezvous.

"There he is," I heard my little sister yelp from somewhere beyond the water fountain. As soon as they were within range, my family hit me with the required volleys of "congratulations" and comments about how classy the ceremony was. The adulation dust was still settling when my father took out his car keys. Traditionally, such a move by my father was an indication that the conversation was definitely over.

"You want to follow us home, son?" he said to me. "Most of the relatives should be at the house no later than five."

Since I had had to be at McCormick Place an hour and a half earlier than my family, my Uncle Elmer had lent me his car. "No, that's okay, Dad. I still have to turn in my cap and gown backstage and that might take a while."

Actually I just wanted to make the trip home alone. There was still a page remaining to be filled in the scrapbook.

Entering the neighborhood and driving blocks out of my way so that I could go down Una's street. As her house came within view, I slowed the car to a crawl. When I was only two houses away I could see that the front door was open. Someone was home. Just as my car approached the front of her house, I caught a glimpse of

Una in the backyard. Not wanting to be seen, I sped up and quickly turned the corner of her street. That graduation day I saw hundreds of people for the last time. Una was one of them.

Driving toward home and the graduation party, still thinking of Una and still presuming we'd get back together again just as we always had. Playing the tough-guy role, even with myself. Trying to convince myself that it didn't matter one way or the other. "What the hell," I said out loud, "I'm young. There'll be plenty of other girls."

And there were. But I was never that young again.